SIX GHOST S

MONTAGUE SUM. ... lish clergyman, occulti... ...ters. His most famous products w ... ...s of colourful studies of vampirism, lycanth..opy and witchcraft, such as *The History of Witchcraft and Demonology* (1926) and *The Vampire: His Kith and Kin* (1928), as well as several volumes of supernatural stories which he edited. He compiled the critical editions of a number of writers, including *Aphra Behn* and *William Congreve*. Alongside these interests, he was also a champion of the English Gothic novel with, amongst other relevant productions, *The Gothic Quest: a History of the Gothic Novel* (1938) and *A Gothic Bibliography* (1941).

DANIEL CORRICK is an editor, philosopher and writer. From 2010 to 2014 he ran Hieroglyphic Press and edited the journal *Sacrum Regnum*. He has published essays on various nineteenth-century figures including Hugo von Hofmannsthal, Gabriele d'Annunzio and Arthur Machen, as well as contributing articles on philosophy of religion topics to the Ontological Investigations blog. He co-edited *Drowning in Beauty: The Neo-Decadent Anthology* (Snuggly Books, 2018).

SNUGGLY BOOKS

MONTAGUE SUMMERS

SIX GHOST STORIES

WITH AN INTRODUCTION BY
DANIEL CORRICK

THIS IS A SNUGGLY BOOK

ISBN: 978-1-64525-007-4

Contents

Introduction

THIS is the first of two volumes collecting the fiction of the Reverend Montague Summers (10 April 1880 – 10 August 1948). The present volume contains *Six Ghost Stories*; the subsequent volume, *The Bride of Christ and Other Fictions*, will contain the remainder of his fictional output.

The name of Montague Summers is familiar to even the modestly well-read aficionado of supernatural fiction. To such he is presented as a picturesque figure—a flamboyant neo-medieval anachronism who believed wholeheartedly in the reality of vampires and werewolves, and who may have had his own dealings with the powers of darkness. He is remembered not so much for what he wrote, but for what he allegedly was, a cross between Bram Stoker's Van Helsing and one of Dennis Wheatley's black magicians. Due to this, it's unsurprising that comparatively few in this scene have actually read anything by Summers as opposed to about him.

This would not have been the case in the pre-war years. For all his occult interests and undoubted piety, Summers' vocation was that of a man of letters, and one who took great relish in macabre and supernatural fiction. As well as being a chief figure in the revival of Restoration Theatre scholarship and a noted historian of the English Gothic—he was responsible for one of the first major histories of that genre and helped republish a number of works—Summers was an enthusiast for that classic nineteenth-century form of horror literature: the ghost story. Such accounts, both those told for entertainment (or notoriety) and of purported real paranormal events, had been an object of fascination for him since childhood, when he apparently witnessed several hauntings in the family home. During the interwar years he compiled three anthologies representative of that genre: *The Supernatural Omnibus*, *Victorian Ghost Stories* and *The Grimoire and Other Supernatural Stories*. His introductions to these volumes, often longer than many of the stories contained therein, provide in-depth accounts of the development of the ghost story from ancient Greece and Rome and in English literature.

They also contain his views on what it is that makes a piece of ghostly fiction successful. Like his more famous namesake, the other 'Monty'—that is M. R. James—Summers holds that modern settings are preferable and that of necessity the ghost must be a creature of malevolence and horror, although he's more willing than the Provost of Eton College to grant room for divinely sanctioned posthumous revenge. Unsurprisingly, he lays more emphasis on requisite belief, or at least entertainment of belief, in the supernatural on the part of the writer and the reader. The metaphysical undertones here link to Summers' broader speculations on the human appetite for dark romantic literature, linking our enjoyment of it both to a religious urge (taken widely enough to include that of the diabolist as well as the saint) and on occasion to sexual masochism.

Ghost story enthusiasts and fans of Summers the man have long regretted that he seemingly produced so little fiction in this vein himself. In his lifetime only three ghost stories from his pen saw publication, two of them, 'The Grimoire' and barely pseudonymous 'The Man on the Stairs', in the last of the above-mentioned anthologies, and the third, a brief vignette 'The Between Maid', which appeared in the *Everybody's Weekly* periodical to which Summers was a frequent contributor throughout the '40s. Biographical material on Summers makes reference to a collection entitled *Six Ghost Stories* announced by the author in the 1938 edition of *Who's Who* as having been sent to publication, but which never appeared nor was heard of again before his death in 1948.

Like so many other projected titles of his, this collection was caught up in the labyrinthine controversies surrounding his dealings with publishers and, after his death, the whereabouts of his unpublished manuscripts. Very briefly: those papers of Summers' not destroyed or stolen immediately after his death were taken by his literary executor and former companion Hector Stuart-Forbes, with the intention of clarifying certain aspects of Summers' ecclesiastical status, only to vanish from sight after Forbes' own death soon afterwards. Fortunately, much of this Nachlass has now been recovered and is available to researchers through the Georgetown University Archives. The introduction to the second volume of Summers' fiction will provide background history for many of these works, but for a general overview of the posthumous manuscript cache and its rediscovery the reader is encouraged to check Gerard O'Sullivan's article 'The Manuscripts of Montague Summers, Revisited'.

Six Ghost Stories does not represent the entirety of Summers' ghostly oeuvre, but the pieces within are undoubtedly his most developed foray into short fiction. The addresses given on some of the manuscripts allow us to date its completion to the last part of the '30s, although the stories originated at the very least a few years earlier. His discussion of the two published pieces in the introduction to *The Grimoire and Other Supernatural Stories*, as well as remarks in his autobiography *The Gallanty Show*, suggest that at least some of them were given as Christmas readings in the company of Sir Edmund Gosse and possibly the poet Arthur Symons and his wife. From recently discovered correspondence, we learn that James himself read and commented favorably on the collection in draft form. It also shows that Summers was actively seeking publishers for the manuscript in 1939, which leads one to wonder whether the *Who's Who* announcement was only wishful thinking on his part (in this period Summers announced several other works including a play about William Henry Ireland, the eighteenth-century Shakespeare forger and a biography of Matthew 'Monk' Lewis, none of which saw the light of day).

10

Stylistically, the pieces are written very much after the manner of the classical Edwardian or late Victorian ghost stories Summers admired so much. Despite its antiquated tone, the prose is relatively restrained; although the phantasms are suitably 'grisly evil things' when finally they make their appearance, much of the time is dedicated to scene setting and narrative background. The heated Gothic prose of his books on witchcraft and vampirism is largely absent in favour of a gradual Jamesian unsheathing of the rhetorical claws. Comparison with those former works and his Catholic symbolist novella *The Bride of Christ* show just how dramatically Summers modified his prose depending on the subject matter.

The influence of James and his master Sheridan Le Fanu can be seen in the pacing and form of the narratives, but the themes are all Summers' own. More than enthusiasm for the occult or Catholic mysticism, it is the idiosyncratic priest's passion for the stage and its lore which informs many of the stories: the loving account of toy theatre dramas and their minutiae reflects Summers' childhood enthusiasm for that forgotten past-time; the ill-fated Romantzini, the 'black Roscius', is based on Ira Aldridge, a sensation of the Victorian stage; and the career of 'La Bressan' reflects the mythologised image European critics constructed around female singers. As is to be expected, there are strong elements of Catholic penitence but also of sexual violence—half the hauntings occur because of the obsession or jealously or revenge of wronged lovers—neither of which would have been tolerated in James's fiction.

We see that that Summers' stories have a more human touch to them than James's, as he dwells less on antiquarian horrors and transgressed boundaries and more on the melodrama proceeding the supernatural climax. Interesting use is also made of colloquial dialogue, often a kind of comic relief in James's work, which Summers expands to an almost stream-of-consciousness level with whole sections of one story being told through a single fragmented run-on conversation.

Summers' eccentric image will probably always loom large over his literary works. The publication of this collection, albeit eighty years later than its author intended, will go some way in vindicating Summers' position not only as a literary historian but also as an enthusiastic practitioner of the English ghost story. Although fiction was not his most prominent vocation, that place being held by his literary scholarship as well as his idiosyncratic occult studies, he warrants a place alongside James, Benson and other figures considered masters of that genre. The release of the second volume in this series will further bolster Summers' reputation as a writer of the dark and spectral as well as reveal his outings into other literary fields.

—Daniel Corrick

A Note on the Texts

OF the six stories in the present collection, four are published here for the first time while two, 'The Grimoire' and 'The Man on the Stairs', were previously published during Summers' lifetime. Those two stories, however, in their previously published form, have many errors and differences from Summers' original manuscripts, which presumably crept in when they were typed up by a hand that was not his own, Summers himself being averse to using a typewriter. The current versions of those stories, therefore, presented in the current volume, have been significantly amended, comparing the previously published versions to the original hand-written versions and, in the case of 'The Man on the Stairs', to an existing typescript as well.

The texts of the remaining four stories, never published before, were taken from individual long-hand manuscripts in the Montague Summers papers collection: Box 3, Folder 8, Georgetown University Library Booth Family Center for Special Collections,

Washington, D.C.; these being the same manuscripts used in the revision of 'The Grimoire' and 'The Man on the Stairs'.

It was Summers' wont to make substantially revisions over the course of a single manuscript meaning a certain degree of editorial interpretation is necessary to make sense of the mass of amendments, deletions and additions; we have kept changes to a minimum and strove to present the stories in the most recent form Summers left them. Though editorial interference has been kept to a minimum, an occasional comma has been added to aid readability.

The publisher and editors would like to thank the staff at the Archives for their invaluable assistance and support, especially Ted Jackson without whom this volume would not have been possible.

Preface by the Author

A LTHOUGH, or perhaps because, I have written introductions to three collections of ghost stories (sixty-six stories), a Preface to the following little volume of half-a-dozen of my own tales in this kind has been called for, and maybe I cannot do better than answer quite briefly a few of the questions which incidentally might arise and some of which indeed have already been asked.

In the first place: the six stories are fiction, not founded upon and not suggested by any personal experience.

Have I any theories or views on the writing of supernatural tales? Frankly, none; or at least none which I have ever been at pains to formulate, and that probably means none which are worthwhile formulating. I have no doubt that the modern critic would be able to supply elaborate directions how to create the proper atmosphere, how to contrive the thrill, when the shudder and the fear must grip tightest, whether the ending should be *rallentando* or startle us out of our senses with a short, sharp bang. But I have noticed that those who are most generous with their recipes are invariably the worst cooks.

There are, of course, certain broad lines upon which any good ghost story (and I suppose any good story for the matter of that) must go, but I cannot think that a writer of fiction consciously observes rules and regulations in his work. It may make it clearer what I intend if I say, for example, that the supernatural has its laws as well as the natural, and our ghosts must and will be found to obey those laws—that is if they are to prove in the least degree convincing, whilst actuality is of the very essence of the ghost story. The tale which wings its flight among chaotic impossibilities and might appropriately have its venue in Cloudcuckootown or Wonderland may be poetical, may be a charming and delightful fantasy, or again a biting satire, but it has no place in the grim world of ghosts, and from the spectral point of view is bound to fail miserably and completely.

When like Owen Glendower we 'call Spirts from the vasty deep', let us be sure that the Spirits are no kindly commonplace apparitions but veritable powers of darkness, grisly evil things of terror and dread and doom, able to send a cold shiver through the reader who sits alone at eleven o'clock on a winter night, and perhaps even to make him hesitate a moment before he switches out the light in bed. The beneficent ghost is (I think) inadmissible because ineffectual in fiction of the gruesome and the macabre, and indeed such friendly visitants belong to altogether another domain of writing.

I would emphasise that unless the stage is well set and the situation made intensely real, ground-work which save in very exceptional cases entails fairly ordinary and not too romantic surroundings with everyday characters, the ghost story goes for naught.

Thus invention must be balanced by fact. In 'Romeo and Juliet' there is no such opera as *I Capuleti e i Montecchi*, as I describe (there is an opera *I Capuleti e i Montecchi*, by Bellini). However, the other operas to which reference is made are all well-known works, and the anecdotes related of Rosa Vitalba and Prete Rosso are true.

There is no such book as the *Mysterium Arcanum*, but *Mystic Divinite* and *A Fountain of Gardens* may be read by those who list.

Places to me are very rich in suggestion. Yet I take it one is at liberty reasonably to change and modify the geography. Silchester is Winchester; Cheriton Manor is a real house, although it is situated not in Essex (as I imagined it) but in entirely another county, and neither story nor legend of any sort attaches to it.

In 'The House Agent' Westbourne is Eastbourne, and I had in mind the neighbourhood of that Sussex watering-place. Caeravon was suggested by a memory of Monmouth a good many years ago; and so on.

I have stated that the six stories are fiction. To be scrupulously exact, in 'The Man on the Stairs' I have ventured to introduce one or two quite minor details of horror which are known to occur in connection with the terrible haunting of a remote old Grange, but as I have just pointed out this is neither a Manor in Essex, nor the actual house I describe.

These must only be taken as a few desultory remarks. Perhaps I have detained the reader too long already, and after all—the proof of the pudding lies in the eating.

Finally, do I believe in ghosts? And have I ever seen a ghost?

The answer to both questions is—yes.

—Montague Summers

SIX GHOST STORIES

The House Agent

O'er all there hung a shadow and a fear;
A sense of mystery the spirit daunted,
And said, as plain as whisper in the ear,
The place is Haunted!
—Hood

IT was eleven-o-clock on a warm June morning when through a fold of the Sussex downs an Alvis Speed Twenty containing two young people swiftly approached the little town of Ringway. Although so far as population is concerned scarcely more than a village—I cannot pretend to know the precise distinction between a large village and a small town, for, when one asks, most people answer to the effect that a town is larger than a village whereas a village is smaller than town, a scrap of information which however accurate and indisputable does not seem to get us very far anyway in our thirst for explicit definitions, and so I invoke the aid of the Oxford Dictionary from which I learn that a town has the complete and independent local government—but this is by the way, and to resume our broken sentence,

Ringway, (which I have heard dubbed 'nothing more than a mere village') whatever the latest census may be, is certainly called a town by its inhabitants and I suppose they ought to know, whilst if a fine old moot hall, its row of timbered cottages, and the twelfth-century church with a real anchorhold count for anything in the balance—and they are good enough at any rate for me—a town it most assuredly is, and, as I am ready and willing to testify, a very pleasant and charming town to boot. There is, indeed, something about it, maybe the soft plane trees that line the silent street, maybe the drowsiness and prim placid quiet that seem to brood eternally over this forgotten little corner of the great world, something which always brings to my lips the missish Victorian phrase 'sweetly pretty'.

This is exactly what Joan Fairgrieve thought although she would have put it in far more modern and trenchant terms. She was feeling particularly happy that morning. They had left tired old London with its noise, its thirsty heat, its crowds and turmoil far behind them, and were bound on the most delightful of quests through the most delightful countryside. Last but not least, she was wearing the most delightful of frocks, and although they had been married quite a long time, nearly twelve months, she was at any rate old-fashioned enough as regards one thing, she still believed it was worthwhile pleasing a husband who continued to be very much in love with her.

'Oh! Dick!' she exclaimed. 'How wonderful! What a perfectly gorgeous place!'

Her husband, whose whole attention was occupied in circumventing a scattered brood of clucking poultry who laboured under the totally erroneous idea that the middle of the road was a safe place for the family to take its matutinal stroll, made no audible reply for a moment. 'M . . . m . . . m . . .' Then he inquired:

'Like to halt here a bit?'

'Oh, yes, rather.'

A few moments later they drew up before the Cat and Wheel, which looked and proved everything an ancient English inn should be. In the tap-room with its low raftered ceiling, flagged floor, settled chimney-place, and deep bay windows whose broad ledge was fragrant with mignonette and made bright with an old painted china jug of flowers, orange and nasturtiums and rustic pastel-coloured stocks, one would not have been a bit surprised to meet Tony Lumpkin in person, ready to knock himself down for a song of Toroddle, toroddle, toroll!

Joan was fairly enchanted with the place, and even Dick confessed himself something more than agreeably surprised to find that Jim Grout the landlord, a fat-paunched scion of the true Stingo line, with his white poll and ruddy gills, kept prime brands of mellow whisky, and although he righteously despised the muck—a sentiment he was at no pains to conceal—was not above mixing a really drinkable cocktail.

'My dear, it's lovely. It's simply lovely.' Thus Joan, perched in a window seat, an Abdulla between her lips.

Dick smiled. 'My dear,' he riposted. 'How many other places during the last month have been simply lovely too?'

'Oh, not like this though. Now, Dick, don't be a brute. I have a presentiment—yes, I have—you needn't laugh at me, Dick Sean, I have a presentiment this is going to be the PLACE!'

'These are rather early days, aren't they, or early minutes—for we've been here a matter of ten minutes at most—to prophesy?'

'Oh, Dick darling,' in a tragic tone, 'don't you like it?'

'Yes, of course, my dear, of course. But we've hardly seen anything of it, have we? Except the bar of this thoroughly jolly pub. Only we aren't going to live in the pub. At least I don't suppose you suggest doing so. Perhaps one might do worse all the same.'

'Don't be so stupid, Dick. You know what I mean. We saw this adorable place as we were coming along.'

You may have, dear. I must acknowledge I didn't see much of it. If these chumps only wouldn't let their damned farm-yard promenade all over the road!'

'Well, anyhow, if you didn't see it you can't talk,' was the devastating reply. 'Now I did . . . and I say it's too wonderful!'

'I can't contradict you, of course. Wouldn't be polite. I only plead that before I sign on a fifty-year lease we may see something more of Ringway.'

'Don't be tiresome,' Joan replied, crushing the stub of her cigarette in an ashtray. 'Naturally we are going to see it. Every hole and corner of it. You are too absolutely Edwardian and argumentative. We are going to start at once, but before we go you can ask that nice fat man to mix me another cocktail. And make up your mind, sir, that you are going to live here . . . here . . . here!'

It will be apparent no doubt from the foregoing conversation that Joan Fairgrieve was more than a little impulsive, as she was also more than a little spoiled by her fond husband, although he not infrequently had to throw cold water on her dazzling schemes, plans which seemed so easy and so absorbing in the first fire of enthusiasm and excitement, but which after cool and tempered discussion proved, alas! utterly impracticable and infeasible.

Yet after half-an-hour's gentle walk through Ringway, after admiring the moot hall from outside and peeping shyly into the old grey church, in reply to his wife's glowing eulogiums Dick went so far as to allow that he thought they very likely had 'struck ile' at last, that they had discovered almost the ideal spot for the weekend cottage which was the aim and object of their peregrinations.

'Only, Joan darling, I haven't noticed anything much to let yet, have you?'

'No . . . no . . .' very hesitantly, 'I can't say I have. But that doesn't mean that there aren't all sorts of delightful places down some of these side streets. They go right off into the country at once, and there are sure to be houses just near. It wouldn't really matter so much if we were five or ten minutes away.'

'I s'pose not. But, Joan, have you thought about electric light and gas? You'd be all right, of course, if you were here—do they call it their High Street or what?—but the further out of the town you get the less likely one would be to find them.'

'Yes . . . I see that . . . it's rather a bore. But then we could manage . . . people *do* manage . . . there are candles, and oil lamps, and oil stoves for cooking. I'll go to the stores tomorrow and find out all about them. I am sure they are perfectly simple to work. Candles too are such fun. You can buy lovely candles nowadays . . . all shades . . . and they make a place look so much nicer . . . candlelight in an old cottage here would be just too lovely!'

'H'm . . . yes . . . perhaps . . .'

'Old brass candlesticks! Oh, Dick, only think of it.'

'I'm afraid they mean an awful lot of work—polishing and all that.'

'But they are effective. Black oak and brass, Dick. That's where the Bunburys made such a mess of it. They haven't anything but oil in their cottage . . . oil lamps and oil for cooking.'

'I expect you'd find there would be oil stoves here— that is unless you were right in the town itself.'

'Oh, lots and lots of people have oil for cooking. Lily Bunbury said it was easy as easy, and so economical!'

'Yes, and do you remember what a vile meal we had that Saturday we motored down to them? Tinned stuff half-warm, and potatoes as hard as bullets, and sopping cabbage.'

'Shall I ever forget it, Dick? But Lily never could cook and never could manage a cook. Besides, they are simply miles from the shops. Here the shops are all right. I've noticed two butchers, and there's quite a large grocer, and a fishmonger's. One ought to be able to get fresh fish here. After all, we cannot be more than five or six miles away from Westbourne and the sea.'

'We should hardly want to go shopping there for week-ends. We could bring stuff with us down from Town.'

'Oh, no, Dick, far better to buy it in the place.'

'Encourage local industry, what?' with a laugh.

'We must order one or two big joints, at any rate. Then they get to like you, and it makes such a difference.'

'I'm afraid even the excellent Dolson would pull a long face if she were asked to cook a big joint over an oil stove down here.'

'I've told you I'll go to the stores and find out all about oil stoves. Yes, I quite see we must think out all these details very carefully . . . I realise how important they are if one's going to be comfortable . . . but then we shall only be here for the summer . . . at first, at any rate . . . and if we like it very very much, Dick,' with a squeeze of his arm, 'as I am sure we shall . . . if we like it very much wouldn't we buy a house here? There's a lovely looking house just beyond the church and it has a board up . . . at least I think it has . . . did you notice it? You can just catch a glimpse of it through the trees.'

'Before we jump too far ahead and talk about buying, Giddy, we had better just find out somewhere if there is anything to let . . . No, that's only a shop and offices above . . . yes, I know it's quaint, but it's no use to us, dear, and there's no earthly good in looking at it. Time is slipping along too . . . we may have to go into Westbourne. I very much doubt if there's a House Agent on the spot, and I suppose that's the nearest likely place.'

'Why not ask the landlord at the Cat and Wheel, Dick? He looks as if he had lived here forever, and I bet you anything he knows the ins and outs of the place, if anyone does. He'll know if there are any houses going.'

'That's a bright idea, Joan. Come along.'

No, Jim Grout couldn't mind anything at the moment that would suit the lady and gentleman. Rare little to be had there was in these parts and that's all there was about it. To be sure, Thirty-two, Mercy Street was empty. Where old Tom Marsh used to be, him as went to live in Brighton along with his married daughter—she's a widow now, lets lodgings and does very well, so it's said. But No. 32 was a shop—corn-chandler old Tom had been—and he supposed that wouldn't do. No, he thought not. What was the house at the backside of the church? Ah, Barton Old House, that was Lady Reculver's place. She died nearly a couple of years ago, and it had stood without a soul in it ever since. A pity—ah, it was that. Ringway had a sad loss of her. Ninety-nine when she died, and right up to the Christmas before her death distributed coals and blankets, and sent round beef and turkeys, and a bottle o' port wine. A fine lot o' stuff, pictures, carpets, books and what not went up to London from t' House, and fetched a reg'lar plum, so he'd heard. Much better have 'em stayed here. But there! My lady was last of the family. There were not many left who remembered her husband, Sir John Reculver, either. Spruce old chap, such as you don't see now-a-days. Above six foot in his socks. A figure of a man, he was. Wore Dundreary weepers until the very end. Many a time had he stopped here when he was on his way to hounds and drunk a cherry brandy. Punctual as clockwork. Never stood for any nonsense, he didn't, and would lend a fellow a clout as look at him, if he were crossed. Quite right too. Never missed a Sunday morning at church. The squire's pew always full. 'Twore one of the good old sort, solid and square. That was in Passun Surale's time. The pew's gone now. And Sir John liked to see the other pews full too. Used to come round on a Monday and ask why the devil you weren't in church . . . straight out, just like that. Never minced about what he had to say to you. And then we all waited in church until t' House party had gone out first, at end of service. Things are altered now that they are, and not for the better, at least not to Mr. Grout's way of thinking.

But, drabbit! How he'd been running on! Still it was cheery once in a way to meet someone who was interested in t' House. Why wasn't it sold? Well, he didn't rightly know as to that. There had been one or two after it at first, but not lately. He minded a chap who had stayed at the Cat and Wheel two or three nights. He talked a lot about the linen-scroll panels. Seemed he was after them more than after the house. O' course there's no denying that neither Sir John nor my lady would ever have the electric put in for one thing. And then the kitchens were a precious sight too large. It would be a costly job putting the electric in now, he reckoned. Mean pulling the place about. Well, you must move with the times a bit, mustn't you? Why, if Mr. Grout hadn't got the electric in here, on the stairs, bedrooms, and all, where would he be? He hadn't suggested t' House to the lady and gentleman because the gentleman said he wanted a smallish place . . . weekend, that's right. Where was the nearest House Agent? Why, it would be at Westbourne or Pudsey. Quite a short ride in a motor car, either of them. Westbourne was a big place. But today young Mr. Verner from Westbourne would be at his office here in Ringway until three-o-clock, at least he dared say, Lord keep his head! Why hadn't he thought of that before! Young Phil Verner of Verner and Randall the House Agents at Westbourne, and if there was anything going in these parts he could put them on to it, for sure. He came over twice a week reg'lar, Wednesday and Saturday mornings to collect rents and so forth, like his pa used to do. He'd known him all his life, since he was just a nipper, in fact, and drove over here with his pa. Cambridge he'd been to, and was a steady clean lad, so everybody said. He used to be a little limb with his monkey tricks, and all, did Master Phil. But never no harm. And Mr. Grout punctuated his reminiscences with a slow unctuous chuckle.

Where was the office? He could point it out almost from the door. Go straight along in the direction of the church, turn down Mercy Street, and it's the fourth house to the left. Ground floor. It's got a brass plate,

'Verner and Randall' on the door. House with wire blinds. You can't mistake it. Lunch when you return? Certainly, sir. Now what you would like? Something hot? Perhaps cold *would* eat better this warm day. There's a piece of prime sirloin in the garden and a good ham. Some soup, first. And what about a raspberry tart to follow? Raspberries fresh picked from the garden. Thank you, sir. Of course we can easily get you chops or a steak, or a fowl, if you fancy it. You prefer the cold? Very good, sir, it shall be all ready for you against you get back.

It was not very many minutes later that Richard and Joan Fairgrieve entered the Mercy Street office of Messrs. Verner and Randal. Obeying the sign, 'Walk in,' they pushed open the green baize door and through a second door just beyond they found themselves in a pleasant panelled room of some size, carpeted, and with a few really good prints on the walls. The young man who was busily pushing a register did not for a brief second look up at this entry, but immediately he saw they were newcomers and strangers he rose quickly from behind his desk with a murmured apology.

'I beg your pardon. I say, I am so sorry! I really thought it was only one of my usual Wednesday clientele.'

'You don't often get inquiries here then?' asked Richard.

'Truth to tell, not often. We mostly do that part of the business at Westbourne. But please sit down, and let me know how I can help you.'

'My wife and I are after a weekend cottage in this district. Not necessarily a large place by any manner of means, but just somewhere to which we can run down from Town with a friend or two. Say four or five bedrooms, dining room and lounge.'

'I understand exactly. In the first place, you must be near here, Ringway?'

'Rather. Is there anything in the town itself?' cried Joan impetuously.

'I'm almost afraid not Mrs. . . . eh . . . oh, thank you,' with a glance at the piece of pasteboard Dick handed him, 'Mrs. Fairgrieve. The houses are either too large for your purpose——'

'Like Barton Old House.' broke in Joan.

'Like Barton Old House. You've seen it then? Exactly. Or else they are not what you want. Rooms over shops and offices. Very convenient and cosy many of them. But definitely not weekend, I should say. You want a garden, of course. Now if you will go out a bit, Westbourne way, only a matter of four or five miles I can give you dozens of bungalows. Any good?'

'Not a scrap, I don't want a fungoid bungalow. I want an old cottage.'

'I see. I won't say it's impossible, but difficult, if you don't half-a-mile or so from here, it makes things much easier.'

'That'll be all right, won't it Dick? But the nearer the better.'

Phil Verner reached for a ledger from a shelf at his side, and began to turn over the pages industriously. 'How does this sound . . . ?' As always there were the houses which were too large, and the houses which were too small.

'We should never get into Rosemary Cottage,' complained Joan, 'and we don't want to keep up Bankside—eight bedrooms.'

'Yes, it's roomy'.

'Besides it's modern, you say.'

'Well, about 1860,' acknowledged Verner.

'Beastly!'

'Oh, it's not at all a bad house, I assure you.'

'I should hate it. So would you, Dick, wouldn't you?'

It will be superfluous to detail the discussion that followed, but at least Verner was able to supply the particulars of five houses of the smaller type all of which he urged it was well worthwhile their seeing. 'I can let you have the keys of the three I have marked with a cross, since they are empty. The other two are occupied, but of course you can see over them. No, it shouldn't take you a great time to go the round of the lot, since you have your car. Suppose I number them in the most convenient order. Five is near Appleton so it is a straight run back here. How long? Oh, only a very few minutes.'

'Now, Joan, come along. It's a good thing we ordered a cold lunch.'

'Where are you lunching? At the Cat and Wheel? My old friend and pal Grout is quite one of our local institutions. You'll find he'll do you very well.'

'Joan, what *are* you staring at?' For his wife was intently examining one of the pictures hanging on the wall.

'Only look, Dick. Three Gates Farm! Isn't it jolly? Oh, how I wish we could find a house like that!'

The print, which was dated 1800, showed a long low building of nearly a couple of centuries before. Two storied, it was removed from any suspicion of squatness by the picture's queer gables and sombre bell-tower. The ivy-clad porch gave on to a narrow stone terrace with a balustrade having urns or balls at the corner, evidently a later addition. Beyond, gently sloped a lawn. From its appearance the place might have been a small manor or a town house before it descended to a farm.

'Does it still exist? Where is it?' queried Joan.

Verner looked at her rather curiously for a moment, 'Three Gates Farm! Oh yes, it's still there.'

'Where?'

'Four and a half miles from here.'

'I suppose it has been knocked about dreadfully, and improved and ruined.'

'No. As a matter of fact it is practically the same as you see it in the print. That's rather a scant impression by the bye. In the interests of business,' with a smile, 'I am keen on old prints!'

'Who lives in it?' catechised Joan.

'Nobody at present.'

'It's empty! Oh! Would they let it?'

'Well, it is to let, but——'

'Oh! Mr. Verner! To let! Dick, *do* let us see it. We *must* see it. How does one get to it?'

'Actually it lies down the Appleston road a mile and a bit further on than Castaly. Yes, the last house on your list, number five. But really Three Gates is an isolated sort of place, and I don't think you'd——'

34

'Isolated! Why, it's only a mile further on you say, and what's a mile in a car! Dick, we simply must see it.'

'Is there anything wrong with the house? Drains?' asked Dick abruptly, a trifle piqued at Verner's slight hesitancy.

'The drains, so far as I know, are in perfect order.'

'Any reason why we shouldn't see it then?'

'Not the slightest,' answered Verner quickly, for his client was showing himself a trifle brusque. 'But,' he added apologetically, 'I'm afraid I haven't got the keys. They are over at Westbourne.'

'Well, how can we get them?'

'Are you returning to Town today? Oh, that's unfortunate, because I can't get away from here until after four—I've an appointment—and I have to put in two or three calls on my way home. My father will have left the office before I get back, and so I shan't be able to put my hands straight away on the Three Gates keys. They will have to be looked out for too, for I don't know exactly where they are. I'm sorry.'

'We needn't go back this afternoon, that's all,' cried Joan. 'Let's stay til tomorrow, Dick; I'm sure we shall be in heaven at the Cat and Wheel anyhow. I know our nice fat friend will rise to a perfectly gorgeous dinner. Oh! It *will* be fun!'

'Why, yes,' replied Dick, 'if Mr. Verner can promise us the keys tomorrow morning we might manage it all right. But we mustn't be late. Remember, Joan, the Archers are dining with us. What time tomorrow could you let us have the keys by, Mr. Verner?'

'Would half past ten do? I'll make a point of sending them over by one of our clerks.'

'Fine. It won't take us long to see Three Gates, and we shall be making a clear start by twelve or just after at latest. That's settled then. You'll be sure to be punctual?'

'You can rely on me. Our Mr. Baker shall meet you outside Three Gates tomorrow morning at 10:30, sharp. I don't think, mind you, that you are going to like the house after all, but——'

'After all, that's *our* business,' interrupted Dick. 'We'll make the appointment definitely. Now, Joan, this time you *must* come along. I'm fearfully hungry. Thanks very much. Good morning.'

'Good morning, Mr. Verner,' echoed Joan.

'Good morning. You'll see me tomorrow, and meanwhile I hope you'll have a good look at those other houses. I'm sure you'll find something among them which will be just what you want. Good morning, Mrs. Fairgrieve!'

As they turned out of Merecy Street Joan took her husband's arm. 'I suppose,' she said confidentially, 'we'd better have a look at—view is the right word, isn't it?—those places this afternoon, Dick, but I know I'm not going to like them. I feel that Three Gates is the house for me.'

'Better wait till we've seen it, dear, at any rate. We don't even know the rent yet. Forgot to ask him. I wonder why he tried to put one off it!'

'Did he, Dick? I didn't notice.'

'Perhaps I'm imagining. But he didn't appear very keen on us seeing it.'

'I expect he didn't want the bother of routing out the keys and sending over—Mr. . . . who was it?—along with them for us.'

'Very likely. Nice sleepy sort of life they lead down here. Makes 'em lazy. Think they can boss the whole place like that old chap Fatty was gassing about—what's his name—Sir John something. But it's not business. They want to be shaken up, that's why I'm determined to see Three Gates. Give a little bit of trouble for once, Mr. Verner' got to put himself out to oblige—good for him. And now—thanks be to Heaven—lunch, at last!'

At the same moment in his office Phil Verner who (if Dick Fairgrieve had really known) was anything but lazy and not a bit inclined to boss stood in front of the print of Three Gates, and as he fingered his chin meditatively he murmured to himself: 'Wonder what the guv'nor 'll say?'

The five highly recommended houses were religiously 'viewed' by Dick and Joan during the course of the afternoon. An excellent lunch at the Cat and Wheel not to mention sundry tankards of Sussex ale tended to make the former a little drowsy, and in this pleasant mood he acquiesced more readily than otherwise he might have done in his wife's withering criticisms of Beechcomb, Myrtle Cottage, and Castaly. The first was not at all what they wanted—here Joan disdained to enter into details—damp or a shrewd suspicion of damp damned Myrtle Cottage, whilst Elsam closets rendered Castaly quite impossible. The two occupied houses provoked even more scathing comment. 'Dick, *did* you see those perfectly awful oleographs in what they called their spare bedroom? And the knotted antimacassars? As for the other place . . . well, all I have to say is that I shouldn't like to have to ask Dobson to sleep in that attic . . . I should expect him to give me notice on the spot . . . There'd be rats . . . I'm sure there'd be rats . . . And now since we are on the Appleton road couldn't we go along just a little further and see Three Gates . . . It's not very far . . . No, I don't intend to set out at all . . . I know we haven't got the keys, but since we're so near we might as well have a look at it from the outside . . . Oh, thank you, Dick . . . Yes, go slow past the house . . . Now we shall know the way all right tomorrow morning . . . Isn't this part of the country simply too gorgeous? I know we are going to be wonderfully happy here . . . Oh! There it is! . . . go slow, Dick . . . look . . . why it's exactly like the picture . . . Isn't it a dream! . . . You lovely house! But there's somebody there! Yes . . . there is I tell you . . . Oh, Dick, I do hope nobody's taken it before us! Can't you see him now? There he is on the lawn—at least he was a minute ago . . . I saw him quite distinctly . . . A tramp? Not a bit like a tramp. Probably the gardener or a caretaker. They must have somebody to look after things . . . I expect they've got a man who comes in . . . and he doesn't want to lose his job . . . perhaps he's a friend of that Mr. Verner's, he seems to know all sorts of odd people . . . Fatty said he used to be a little limb . . . Depend upon it, that's it. He's put someone in here who's useful to him . . . and of course he doesn't want him turned out, that's why he isn't keen on letting the house . . . Not that I noticed it myself . . . but you said so . . . Three Gates is wonderful! Deserted? Yes, it does look a little deserted, but then it may have been shut up for ages . . . anyhow, it's wonderful.'

Though plain, Mr. Grout's dinner was so admirably cooked as to rouse Dick almost to enthusiasm, whilst he declared it was worthwhile remaining down from London to sample mine host's burgundy alone. 'By Jove,' he cried, 'I don't know when I've felt so peckish. Are you hungry, Joan? I'm as hungry as a hunter.'

'It's the air,' sagely commented Joan, 'it's the Sussex air. The best in England. I've just read all about it in a guide book in the lounge—parlour, I ought to call it—whilst, Dicky Sour, you were swilling sherry in the bar before dinner.'

'Must order something for the good of the house, my dear. And if we are going to live here I can't take too early an opportunity of mixing with the native element.'

Piquet passed a very happy evening, until declaring she was sleepy and must be fresh for Three Gates tomorrow Joan withdrew to bed at an unwonted early hour, leaving Dick to follow after he had rubbed elbows with a few more of the native element in the crowding tap-room and won golden opinions on all sides by freely standing drinks to most the *habitués* of the Cat and Wheel.

✳

Just when Joan was scoring her last capot, half-a-dozen miles away at the Laurels, Melcomb Road, Westbourne, Phil Verner strolled almost too carelessly into his father's study with a 'I don't want to disturb you, dad, but——'

'Well, what is it, my boy?' inquired Mr. Verner Senior, putting a marker in the volume of Swedenborg, his favourite author.

'You know I hate talking business out of hours——'

'And in hours too sometimes, eh, Phil?' chuckled the old gentleman. 'But pleasantry apart, what is it?'

'Nothing really, only this morning at Ringway a couple of people—man and his wife, Fairgrieve their name is—quite decent folk, driving a jolly good car Grout says, came in after a weekend cottage.'

'All depends what they want and where. What of it anyhow, Phil? Surely you've got the register and copies of the list there?'

'Oh, yes, I ladled them out the usual Ringway lot, all we've put down in the books. Castaly, you know, and Beechcomb, and that ghastly Sunny Bank——'

'Ah! You'll be doing old Mrs. Bodkin a kindness if you can persuade anyone to take that.'

'I should think so. But no chance with them. They won't fall for it. They have ideas. I don't fancy Fairgrieve himself would be over particular as long as he were comfortably fixed. He didn't strike me as that sort. But to cut a long story short, the dame——'

40

Mr. Verner raised a protesting hand. 'Again I must ask you, Phil, not to use this slang. You know I don't like it.'

'Sorry, dad. Anyhow Mr. Fairgrieve caught sight of that old print of Three Gates on the wall, and began to rave about it and ask questions.'

The old man, keenly alert, sat up in his chair and set down his book smartly.

'Well . . . I hope you didn't tell her anything?'

'She asked bang out if it was to let, and I had to say yes. What could I do? It *is* to let, you know.'

'I wish as we had never touched that property. And yet in the circumstances how could I have avoided it! The only thing I can do is to keep it empty!'

'Hang it all! Dad, I don't see why because there's been a murder in a house years ago it's got to be shut up for ever. There must have been murders in heaps of houses people are living in quite happily today. Honest, it seems too stupid.'

'It's you who are stupid, Phil, incredibly stupid. But of course you don't understand and perhaps you never will. I hope so for your own sake, I'm sure. At the same time you were fully aware of my wishes on the point, and yet you do this. I am seriously annoyed.'

'I didn't do anything, dad. You can't blame me. I tell you she saw the picture of the place, and how could I answer her when she began cross-examining me? They would have found out sooner or later that it was to let. They are staying the Cat and Wheel tonight, and he'll pick up all the gossip for ten miles round in the bar. Why Grout's a chronicle in himself.'

'That's all very well. And what happened?'

'Nothing would satisfy her but she must go over it. After all, why not?'

Mr. Verner shook his head, and Phil continued: 'I did my level best to put them off it but he sniffed that I was shuffling and he got rather peeved—oh, call it what you like. He was huffed—I could see that anyhow, and he hardly attempted to disguise it either. I didn't want to lose them.'

'Naturally not. I see.'

'So I told them—as was the truth—I hadn't the keys over there. They were going back to London today. Then she said they'd stay and see the house tomorrow. Forced my hand. I promised I'd send the keys across in the morning by ten-fifteen. I thought Baker could take them. Or if you would rather, I'll nip along myself. I've arranged to meet them at Three Gates. Then it won't take too long to see over the place and they want to get back to Town pretty early, at least they said. And that will be an end of the whole thing.'

'I understand. Yes. Anyhow, we can do nothing about it tonight, and so we needn't discuss it any further. Perhaps I did speak rather sharply, Phil, just now. It was a little awkward for you. You want to be as old as I am to know how to manoeuvre ladies when they begin asking questions. Leave it entirely to me. I'll decide what's best to be done. Are you going out this evening?'

'Well, I thought I'd stroll down to the club for a hand at bridge. That is unless you want me?'

'Oh, no. Be off with you, boy. And don't worry.'

'Then I'll say good-night, dad.'

'Good night, Phil.'

As is the way with most town folk after a first night in the country, when one has fallen to sleep between strange sheets listening to such unusual noises as the movement of the drowsy cattle in their sheds, the hooting of an owl, the restlessness of the farm yard annoyed by some unwelcome visitor, Joan not only awoke early, but once her eyes were well open felt it impossible to lie any longer in bed. The consequence was that she and Dick indulged in a stroll, had eaten a hearty breakfast, had glanced through *The Daily Mail* and *The Mirror* and smoked half-a-dozen cigarettes between them, all by nine-fifteen, an hour which at home usually saw her maid entering her room with her morning tea.

They were standing the porch of the Cat and Wheel watching Ringway go about its morning business in leisurely fashion enough when the church clock chimed the half-hour.

'Five and forty minutes before we meet our Mr. What's-his-name at Three Gates, Dick. How about scouting along now and having a good look round the garden, such as it is, and getting the hang of the outside of the house? It'll save time later on.'

'Yes, if you like. Of course we might do that.'

On the way to Three Gates Joan was all fuss and excitement. The house stood fairly close to the road, and to their surprise when they left their car and walked up the drive they saw that the solid nail-studded oak door was half open.

'I believe he's got here before us!' she exclaimed.

'Looks like it,' answered Dick. 'He'd want to come over and open up the place a bit. Air it—let some light in at any rate, for I dare say most of the windows have been shuttered and barred for ages. Place gets mouldy.'

As they entered the hall a man advanced to meet them. He was gaunt and dark, with close-cropped black hair, large black eyes, and a swarthy complexion which gave him something of a gipsy cast of countenance. He looked, they noticed, more like a country farmer than a clerk, being dressed in leather gaiters and a ribbed brown velveteen jacket with a scarlet handkerchief loosely tied round his neck.

'You are from Messrs. Verner, the House Agent? 'Dick queried. 'We've come to have a look round over the house as was arranged yesterday.'

'House Agent! Oh, yes, I'm the House Agent, no one else,' answered the man with a courteous bow in a singularly deep husky voice. 'I shall be very pleased to show you over. Nobody knows the house as well as I do. This way is the dining-room,' and he threw open a door.

'What an odd sort of person to be a House Agent,' whispered Joan clinging on her husband's arm.

'H-s-s-sh! dear, you know in these country places they have to dress to suit their clients. And I daresay most of 'em are country bred themselves.'

The dining-room, large and lofty, with French windows opening upon an unkempt but otherwise fascinating garden walled at the back pleased Joan immensely. She saw illimitable possibilities of old-world flower beds. 'Of course we must have electric light put in here,' she proclaimed as she stood in the corner of the room and took a sweeping survey, 'it will need several points and switches but that's quite easily done. Dick, what a room to have dinner in on warm evenings with those windows open . . . Yes, I know it needs decorating . . . it is in rather a bad state . . . But only think of a table and the windows open on to the garden . . .'

'The windows have been found very convenient before now,' commented their guide.

They proceeded to a second room of ample proportions. 'The living-room,' announced the Agent. This was something old and discoloured in detail. The mantelpiece, Joan, decided, was Adams—or at any rate nearly Adams.

Other rooms were similarly investigated. The kitchen proved, it is true, a bit on the spacious side—you might have roasted an ox under that huge chimney—but Joan came to the rescue with the happy suggestion that it should be turned into a servants' hall—'they want somewhere to sit, especially in the country'—and a gas cooker could be quite simply put in the scullery, itself of no insignificant dimensions, and there you were!

It was on the tip of Dick's tongue to inquire where on earth the gas was coming from, but having no desire to launch out upon further discussion at the moment he discreetly decided to ignore any such awkward little details.

The staircase was not ascended without enthusiastic and truly deserved encomiums, for it was a beautiful piece, black as ebony, although Dick ventured to hint difficulties as to the working of the house. None the less, Joan highly approved of the various bedrooms branching off to the right and left of the landing. 'Practically all of the two floors! How convenient!' she cried.

'This, madam,' said the Agent, 'was the best bedroom where Mr. Cooper and his wife always slept.'

'Ugh . . . and I don't like it at all . . . there's something nasty about it . . . Oh! I could never sleep here . . . don't you feel it, Dick? Perhaps it's that abominable wall-paper. What a pattern! Those huge roses, I suppose they were red once, and the cheap gilt-trellis-work! Thank goodness it's faded.'

'The wall-paper was particularly admired when it was new,' came a gruff voice from the doorway.

'So it may have been! Fifty years ago!' answered Joan, and thought to herself, 'well, he needn't feel so badly about it even if I don't like his awful old wall-paper,' for she caught—or thought she caught—a particularly malignant side-glance from the Agent.

'Yes, it's all quite delightful,' was the final decision, delivered by Joan as they stood in the hall. 'Of course there's a lot wants doing to it—and now what about the rent and things?'

'Look here, dear,' protested Dick, 'don't you think we'd better write Messrs. Verner about that when we get back to Town? Rent, and rates and repairs, and so forth. We can settle all those details later. And you know we do want to be getting along.'

'That's all very well, Dick, but there are hundreds of things about a house which you may never think of. We ought to go over it again. At any rate, I should like to take another look upstairs. I haven't quite mapped out the bedrooms yet and that's so important.'

'Oh! really, Joan if you're going to spend your whole morning looking at empty bedrooms—I'm sorry, I didn't mean that . . . I know it's important . . . you want another squint upstairs . . . All right . . . I don't think I'll come . . . I'll just go down and start up the car . . . you won't be long?'

'Not three minutes,' answered Joan. 'But I would just like to decide how to arrange those four rooms. I hope I'm not keeping you—I'm not taking up too much of your time?'

'Keeping me? Oh, no,' answered the Agent as he preceded her upstairs, whilst Dick rather weary of the whole business crossed the hall and resolutely strode down the drive.

'Here is a room I don't think you've seen yet,' said the Agent. 'Please walk right in.'

'Why, I thought we'd—oh!' cried Joan.

The room into which she was ushered was fully furnished in a dull mid-Victorian fashion. There was a large double bed overlaid with a patchwork quilt; a clumsy great wardrobe; a dressing-table of no small size, encumbered with a toilet set in painted china—trinket trays, vases, bottles, and a pair of those extraordinary antlered stands which Joan noticed were hanging with thick tawdry rings; a double washstand; a horse-hair sofa and chairs upon which it appeared impossible that anyone should sit, at least in any comfort or security.

'Why . . . why . . .' stammered Joan as a sharp thrill of fear ran through her.

'That wall-paper! . . . oh!'

The wall-paper was bright and glossy, as though it had been pasted yesterday, with a hand pattern of glaring red roses clambering around a cheap gilt trellis. . .

'This is the room where the murder was done,' said the Agent. He was standing with folded arms, his back to the door, glowering down at her.

'Murder!' screamed Joan, thoroughly frightened. 'Oh! The man is mad . . .' she thought. 'Dick! Dick! Where is Dick!'

'Ay, and a bloody bad murder it was too. Did you never hear of it? It made a noise at the time . . . I don't 'xactly remember how long ago. Tom Cooper murdered his wife here. Don't you want to hear about?'

'No . . . no . . . no!'

'A light woman, she was. But he loved her for all that. Oh yes, he loved her sore and cherished her. He bought her all this fine furniture . . . and it cost a tidy penny too! That's the wardrobe where she would hang her frocks . . . ah! and the bright looking-glass . . . many's the time she sat in front of it, combing out her pretty hair, and thinking of—her lovers, maybe. For she had lovers a score . . . a light woman, she was . . . so he set to kill her—her husband set to kill her . . . Now, I ask you, there was naught else to do, was there? And he killed her, he did. He throttled her. He had his fingers round her slim white throat, and tugged . . . and

48

tugged . . . and tugged . . . Tom Cooper did. They got him for it though—they wouldn't listen to what he had to say, judge nor all . . . not a word . . . though he told 'em again and again . . . she was a light woman, he said . . . but they hanged him in Lewes gaol . . . See here!' and the Agent twisting the scarlet handkerchief from his throat showed a hideous swollen and distorted neck, ribbed with deep purple weals as his head suddenly fell on one side, the eyes almost started from their sockets, and his huge tongue lolled aimlessly out.

'A bleedin' whore she was . . .' the voice sounded far away '. . . went with Dan'l Coates the cowherd so she did . . . I caught 'um at it down yonder in the byre . . . "in the very act," the Good Books says . . . a bleedin' whore . . .'

The horrible thing advanced slowly in the direction of Joan, its long lithe sinewy fingers crooking towards her throat . . . It was on her . . . She felt its clay cold touch . . . the stink of its fetid breath . . .

Dick was beginning to grow a little impatient. He wished Joan wouldn't be so long. He doubted whether Three Gates was quite the place for them in any case. All right if you were going to live in it most of the year . . . but much too large for a weekend. And it sounded very simple to talk about putting in electric and gas . . . but those things cost money . . . and unless you bought outright, was it worthwhile? Of course, Joan was keen on it, and that mean a great deal. But, bless her! She hadn't a business head . . . God Lord! Why must she go back and dawdle round those bedrooms! Measuring for carpets and curtains he wouldn't be surprised just like her!

This was too much of a good thing! They must be getting along, and he supposed he'd have to go back and fetch her out.

To his surprise Dick Fairgrieve found the solid nail-studded oak door, which he was sure he had left standing wide open closed, and all his shouting and banging, even when he took a stone from the garden and hammered with might and main awoke not the slightest response.

Growing seriously alarmed he ran along the terrace round to the back of the house and regardless of consequences smashed in the glass of a French window, which at any rate gave him a rough entry. They had been in that room, he knew, but the door was now locked although as he pulled and kicked the look noisily ricocheted asunder.

He called. There was no answer. The rooms all seemed dusty and deserted. A cold fear at his heart, he took the stairs three at a time, and threw open the first to which he came. It was the best bedroom. From the walls there hung peeling tattered strips a faded paper of red roses trailing over a screen of cheap gilt trellis. There in the centre of the floor lay the dead body of his wife, her face bloodless, her wide eyes staring unspeakable agony and dread, and her hair, her radiant blonde hair, white as snow.

❄

At the same moment Jim Grout at the Cat and Wheel was taking a telephone message from Westbourne: 'Verner and Randall . . . Mr. Verner . . . Mr. Verner senior speaking . . . Will you please tell Mr. Fairgrieve that it is impossible for us to let him have the keys, as arranged, of Three Gates Farm. Yes; I am sorry, but it is quite impossible. In fact, so far as we are concerned, the house has been definitively withdrawn from the market.'

The Governess

Up through the wather your secret rises;
The stones won't keep it, and it lifts the mould,
An' it tracks your footsteps, and yoar fun surprises
An' it sits at the fire beside you black and cowld.

Ballad of Tim Rooney
—Le Fanu

'THE stupid woman!' And folding the letter back into its envelope my aunt laid it down on the little pile by her side, delicately took off her gold spectacles, returned them to their case, and drank another sip of tea.

'Who, aunt?' I queried between two mouthfuls of grilled sausage.

'Why—Lady—Lady—Lady—what's her name?—Lady Hangood-Ash.'

'And who is Lady Hangood-Ash?'

'Well, my dear, you know as much about that as I do myself. Really her name conveys nothing at all

52

to me. She reminds me that I met her last winter in London at your cousin Olivia's.'

'At one of Olivia's crushes? I quite agree. She must be extraordinarily stupid to allow herself to be drawn into one of those.'

'I didn't intend that at all. Whatever else Olivia is, she is extremely good-natured. Of course there's no denying she does contrive the most miscellaneous conversaziones.'

'Someone said her aristocratic drawing-rooms are just like a pack of cards without the kings and queens.'

'What do you mean?'

'All knaves and commons.'

'That's very unkind. At the same time, I wish Olivia wouldn't be so effusive in her introduction . . .'

'Let's drop Olivia. Of course she'd hate it if she knew. She loves being talked about . . . but what news of milady?'

'Oh! Lady Hangood-Ash. Well, I give you my word, my dear, I haven't the slightest recollection of meeting anyone of that name, and here she writes asking me to recommend a school for her two daughters. Why on earth should she imagine I know anything about schools?'

'Olivia told her. Aunt, your marmalade is excellent.'

'You could get it just as easily as I do, dear, if you chose. Cooper's, Oxford.'

'Somehow I never remember.'

'You're lazy.' I protested inarticulately and vainly. 'Yes, you are, Tony. You've got a lazy memory. Oh, yes,

I know you'll work all day long at the British Museum or the Bodleian, and bury yourself in books from cock-crow to sunset——'

'Neither the British Museum nor the Bodleian opens at cock-crow.'

'Don't jape. I was using a figure of speech. But when it comes to a thing like marmalade—a small item but one which makes for comfort and content—why, you're all at sea.'

'Yes, aunt, but marmalade always tastes so much better here than anywhere else.'

'Butter, my dear.'

'No, marmalade.'

'Are you going to persist in being clever—or stupid, is it? Over the breakfast table, Tony?'

'It's too early for either, aunt. Let us consider the case of Lady Hangood-Ash. No doubt Olivia told her that you were President of the Board of Education, or at least the power behind the throne—or whatever the Board sits on.'

'Olivia takes a good deal too much on herself,' replied my aunt rather testily—that is for her—as she glanced again at Lady Hangood-Ash's letter.

'Why an old woman of nearly seventy—yes, I am nearly seventy, and it's no use saying "nonsense," Tony—an old woman of nearly seventy just because until fifteen odd years ago she kept an old-fashioned school——'

'A college, aunt.'

'Oh, yes, I know they call it a college now, but a school it was in my day, and a school it will remain for me. Why an old woman who has retired to Cheltenham and peace should be compelled to advise all her acquaintances and all her relatives' acquaintances how and where to educate their children I just don't know.'

'Especially when she doesn't approve of modern education at all,' I murmured.

'Especially when she doesn't approve of the so-called modern education at all,' concurred my aunt. 'Why I read in the papers only the other day that some brazen educationalist—a female, of course—was urging that there should be classes for girls to teach how to buy smart frocks, and how to make up, plaster their faces all the colours of the rainbow. Ugh! I shouldn't wonder if there weren't university courses to teach women to walk the streets before long. I expect there are already if we only knew—in Russia. I shall write to Lady Hangood-Ash and tell her that the most sensible thing she can do is to keep her two daughters at home and provide them with a strict governess.'

'So you think that's the best system, aunt?'

'In most cases, my dear, yes, Of course it doesn't always turn out well . . . you have to be careful whom you admit to your house, and I remember a curious story . . . but then it all happened so long ago, and I don't believe anyone even really knew the right of it.'

'Right of what, aunt?'

'Oh, it's an old story, my dear, and I don't want to be bothering you with it.'

'You know I love your stories, aunt.'

'Very well then, remind me after dinner tonight and you shall hear.'

And this is the story my aunt told.

✻

In the handsome and spacious library at No. 27 Harley
Crescent, St. John's Wood, N.W., wearing a look of the
most poignant distress and a rich citron moiré silk—it
was frequently debated amongst her friends whether in
spite of her coal-black hair a lady of such ample bust
and florid complexion was not a little unwise in her
constant choice of the bolder colours—Mrs. Professor
Brassington, as she insisted upon being called, was
seated opposite her husband, whose somewhat noncha-
lant appreciation of the present crisis seemed to cause
that worthy matron the liveliest concern, and when she
spoke it was in a tone of the utmost irascibility.

'Really, Professor, how you can sit there and smile,
yes, actually smile when you see me so vexed and wor-
ried, I can't for the life of me imagine!'

'Why, my dear,' announced the Professor in his
bland unctuous voice, gently placing the tips of his
fingers together—a favourite gesture. 'Why, my dear,
what would you have me do? And I'm sorry I smiled. I
am sure I didn't intend it. My thoughts were far away.'

'That's just what I complain of, your thoughts always are far away, and if I didn't toil and moil and think
for us both I am positive this house would never go on
at all. Now pray do give me five minutes of your time.
I hope that's not too much to ask.'

'I'm all attention, my dear.'

'Miss Taylor is leaving us on Wednesday week.'

'So I understand.'

'Most inconsiderate I call it after all these years. And I am sure she's been treated just as if she were one of the family. Thoroughly inconsiderate and selfish.'

'I believe she is going to be married, my dear.'

'So she says.'

'You've no reason to doubt it?'

'Oh, no, none at all. But what does she want to get married for I should like to know? In any case, she should perfectly well have waited until the end of the summer.'

'True, my dear. Only so far as we are concerned I am afraid the problem which lies before us would have been just the same then as now.'

'I don't know anything about that. As you are well aware, Professor, I'm not one to be looking forward to trouble and difficulties. Anyhow she *is* going to be married in a fortnight's time, and that's all there is to it. Of course I asked her to postpone her wedding, but would she? Oh, dear me, no! It seems the man she's engaged to—she's been engaged for years and I never so much as suspected it!—is going out to India. To India!'

'A very wealthy and promising country.'

'What has that to do with it? The fact remains she refuses to oblige me—after all the kindnesses I've shown her too! But there! Do I ever meet with anything but thanklessness! Well, she's off on Wednesday week and here we are in a perfect quandary. For where to find another governess for Frieda, I just do not know.'

'Where did you get Miss Taylor?'

'She came from Lady Lavenham.'

'Oh yes, of course, I recollect now. I wrote to Horsley and he put us in touch with her.'

'Not that Lady Lavenham would have recommended her for a moment had she known she was going off like this to get married.'

'But it must be nearly five years ago, my dear, that Miss Taylor first came to us.'

'And doesn't that make it all the worse? Frieda is just at the age now when it's most important that she should be progressing along a continuous course of study. Not all this chopping and changing. A girl turned fifteen wants a steady influence. It's an awkward time. There's her music. And then her languages. And her social training, which is *so* important. How to hold herself, how to enter a room—a hundred and one points of etiquette. Miss Taylor would have done all that so well. You yourself said her manners were particularly good. And now she disappoints us all like this! Oh, dear! Oh, dear! Whatever shall we do?'

'Advertise, my dear.'

'Advertise!'

'Yes, certainly, advertise in *The Times* or *The Morning Post*, and meanwhile I'll keep my eyes and ears open and I may pick up something from one of my colleagues just as Horsley introduced us—in the first place—to Miss Taylor.'

At first Mrs. Brassington refused to answer so simple a way out of her difficulties. She felt that the problem should not have been solved that easily. There should have been a good deal more embarrassment and perplexity, multifold exasperation, giving her as wide a scope as possible for self-pity and the most voluble self-laudation. But when the Professor, who was indeed inured to such dilemmas, refused to be shaken out of his normal calm and to ask her prophecies and unerringly presented a front of stoic philosophy she gradually came round to his suggestion, and, in fact, within twenty-four hours had so far as adopted it—that she was proclaiming herself as the originator of the idea which she was sure would produce the happiest results.

'Of course,' she confided to a friend, 'the Peplors found an excellent governess through the medium of an advertisement. She could speak four—or was it five? —languages fluently—or was that the butler who ran away with the plate whilst they were in the South of France? I forget which, but anyway Mrs. Peplor told me herself that it was almost satisfactory. Dr. Masters, too, secured a first-class governess through an advertisement. Later on he did discover there was something between her and young Jeff Masters—yes, the youngest son—and strictly *entre nous*, although he said it came to nothing serious I shall always believe—well, my dear, that a little stranger arrived on the scene—you understand me—but of course we haven't any sons and so nothing of the sort could happen with us.'

The work of opening the batches of letters which were received in answer to the advertisement, of checking them, reading them, sorting and selecting them, fell of course to the Professor. He also it was who conducted the preliminary inquiries. When references had been taken up and the list sifted Mrs. Brassington—exclaiming that everything had fallen upon her shoulders—assumed the rôle of final arbiter—strictly speaking—arbitrarily.

There was a good deal of necessarily tiresome business—there were many disappointments and set-backs on both sides—that it was about two weeks after the first insertion of the advertisement that the Professor came into lunch from his study walking pretty briskly, and rubbing his hands together in token of his complete satisfaction.

'Well, Professor?' queried his lady who recognised the signs.

'Well, my dear—ah! what have we here? An omelette! Stewed kidneys and mushrooms! Excellent—well, my dear, I think we've found a governess at last.'

'I'm very pleased indeed to hear that. Not but what one of so many applicants—how can—Now have you gone into all the details carefully? Have you explained to her exactly what she will be expected to do? Have you taken up the references?'

'To your two first questions, my dear, yes. To your last, I shall write to Lady Fitzowen immediately after lunch.'

'Lady Fitzowen?'

'Yes. That is the reference she gave. Lady Fitzowen, Shanklin Castle. The Fitzowens have had Shanklin since the fifteenth century. It is an historic place. With a reference like that it can't go wrong.'

'It sounds respectable at any rate,' quoth Mrs. Professor Brassington. 'When are we going to see her, and what is her name?'

'I have appointed Miss Catherine Howard to call here at five-o-clock this afternoon, if it suits you, my dear.'

'I will make it suit me, Professor.'

Miss Catherine Howard passed with glowing colours even the ordeal of Mrs. Brassington's capable scrutiny. She was beyond all question—not merely ladylike—but, to use her employer's phrase, 'a lady'; she answered the Professor's inquiries in French, German and Italian with perfect ease in the same languages; she was not servile but civil; she carried herself well and acknowledged without boasting her ability to teach music—beyond the point which Frieda was ever likely to reach—dancing, deportment . . . undoubtedly she had more accomplishments than the Vicar's daughters who could 'pinch, point and frill; unfasten their needle, cross-stitch, cross and change, and all manner of plain-work; could do up small cloths and work upon catgut; could cut paper, and had a very pretty manner of telling fortunes upon the cards!'

In appearance Miss Howard was tall and svelte; quiet and almost subdued in her manner, answering all questions in a low singularly sweet voice, and scarcely raising her fine grey eyes from the ground. Her oval face, which struck one by its unusual pallor, was framed in masses of auburn hair neatly braided under a dark bonnet—you must remember this was nearly fifty years ago.

'Well, Miss Howard,' announced Mrs. Brassington with her hand on the bell-pull at the conclusion of half-an-hour's inquisition, 'assuming that we receive a satisfactory reply from Lady Fitzowen——'

'As I have no doubt will be the case,' suavely interjected the Professor, with a courteous old-fashioned inclination.

'Assuming that we receive a satisfactory reply from Lady Fitzowen, we shall have no hesitation in engaging you for this important post—the education of our daughter—our only daughter. Lumsdon, the door.'

Miss Howard bowed and passed from their presence.

'Very suitable, Professor, very suitable. I confess I shall feel quite easy in mind if I secure her. I really think I may congratulate myself on my choice—and even you will allow that I don't often go wrong in my judgement of character. It's fortunate I can sum up a person as well as anyone. Did you notice what good material her gown was made of? No? Well, of course you never notice anything. The basque, perhaps, is a little old-fashioned—the season before last—but that doesn't matter in a governess, indeed it's a good thing—but the cut was perfect. I wonder where she gets her clothes? Oh, I suppose being a governess she made them at home. Why, I might allow her to cut out a dress for me! Well, we shall see.'

A reply from Lady Fitzowen, written on thick creamy note-paper stamped with Shanklin Castle, arrived in due course. Miss Howard was spoken of in letters of the highest commendation, and Mrs. Bressington herself wrote off the same afternoon to engage the new governess.

It was on the evening of Thursdays, April the eighteenth, that Miss Howard in a fly with a couple of humble trunks arrived at No. 27 Harley Crescent. A schoolroom tea—ham and eggs, hot scones, marmalade and strawberry jam, for Mrs. Brassington boasted a liberal table—awaited her, good solid fare for which both she and her pupil Frieda, whose acquaintance she now made for the first time, did ample justice.

Frieda was a slim girl of nearly sixteen, one who would never be in any sense beautiful nor really pretty but who when her rather angular contours had filled out might become distinctly attractive since she had fine eyes, fine teeth, and a fine skin. Rather shy, very romantic, and exceedingly given to reading Ouida's novels in private, she was ready to fall instantly in love with any new face, and by the end of the evening had prepared herself to give Miss Howard her fullest confidence, harmless confessions enough which she was surprised to find were rather checked than encouraged.

This did not prevent, in fact it rather incited Frieda to become fired with an ecstatic devotion to her new governess, although that lady invariably repressed any attempt at demonstration, and to use Mrs. Brassington phrase—'held herself aloof'. Not that she ever showed herself disinclined to fulfil any one of her duties—to come down to the drawing-room and play the piano when there came guests for dinner, to write a letter of two for Mrs. Brassington, to address the envelopes for the next at-home, to take a hand at whist, or even to make one at the dinner-table when owing to influenza poor Mrs. Lethaby failed them at the last moment. But as Mrs. Brassington expressed it: 'you never seem to get any further with her. And I'm sure I've tried often enough.'

It was Frieda's custom, after she had risen at half-past seven, dressed, turned her mattress, spent ten minutes in private devotion and thereafter open her window according to the ritual Mrs. Brassington presented, before she descended to the breakfast-room—the matriarch approved of breakfast being taken by all four in common at nine-o-clock, preceded by prayers which she herself declaimed from an ancient but stately Book of Family Worship—to visit Miss Howard's room about a quarter before the hour.

The governess was almost invariably dressed, and often would be seated at the open window, reading, although once or twice Frieda found she had not quite completed her toilet and was fastening her cuffs or collar when she cried 'come in' to the accustomed knock on the door. It was on one of these occasions that Frieda noticed she looked pale-faced and heavy-eyed, and contrary to her wont it was only with a faint wan smile she greeted her pupil.

'Oh, Miss Howard! Aren't you well?' cried Frieda, all alarm. 'Let me ask Mother to send your breakfast up? Just a boiled egg and a cup of tea.'

'Nonsense, Frieda, I'm quite all right,' was the reply. 'I had rather a bad night—dreams—or rather nightmares.'

'Well, I hardly know what it is to dream—unless I've eaten too much supper the evening before—and then it's dreadful.'

Miss Howard who was fastening her belt before the looking-glass made no immediate reply. Then, 'Would you please give me a clean handkerchief, Frieda?' she asked. 'They are in the wardrobe, the bottom tray. You'll find them in that green quilted sachet.'

Delighted to be of service to her beloved Miss Howard even in the most trifling way, Frieda at once opened the wardrobe and found the required article.

'What a lovely scent,' she exclaimed.

'Yes, it's rather nice. It's the pot-pouri sewn in the sachet.'

'Here is your handkerchief, Miss Howard. But—oh! however did that happen? It's all wet! And I'm sure I didn't drop it! Why, it's sopping wet! Oh! I hope I haven't spilt a bottle of scent or anything in the wardrobe!'

To her surprise Miss Howard snatched the handkerchief out of her hand and flung it into the corner of the room. Her face had grown deadly white, and as she gripped the edge of the dressing-table her knuckles showed bloodless and blanched.

'No . . . no . . . there's nothing spilled . . . At least I don't suppose so . . . Get me another handkerchief, Frieda, please . . . is that all right . . . quite dry?'

'Oh, yes, I think so. Yes,' answered the astonished girl holding out a second small square of fabric.

'Thank you, dear. I'm sorry if I startled you a little. My nerves . . . I don't feel very well this morning.'

'Then do let me ask for a cup of tea in your own room.'

'No . . . certainly not . . . It's nothing . . . There's the breakfast gong! Come, Frieda, your mother will wonder why we are late.'

Throughout the day all passed tranquilly enough. About eleven-o-clock the next morning Mrs. Brassington summoned Miss Howard from the schoolroom to her boudoir, as she insisted upon it being called.

'Oh, Miss Howard,' she said turning from the little walnut escritoire at which she was seated vainly endeavouring to cope with a pile of accumulated correspondence, 'I am so sorry to interrupt your lessons—but here's this letter—apparently it came last night, when as you know the Professor and I were out at the Royal Society—at any rate it's too tiresome, Mrs. O'Connall writes she will be unable to dine with us this evening. She is called back over to Ireland. I wonder what for indeed! It puts my whole table out . . . fortunately she is a widow or we should be two places short . . . anyhow it's too late to ask anyone else so will you please dine downstairs this evening . . . at 7.30, but, of course you needn't come into the drawing-room until ten minutes before . . . and I really don't know with whom I can send you in to dinner . . . but I'll find someone . . . you'd better wear that pretty blue frock of yours . . . yes, the one with the silver sequins . . . charming . . . Thank you . . . and how is Frieda progressing? . . . Yes; well I'd better not detain you from your studies any longer.'

The dinner party was all that a dinner party of 1890 would be. Elaborate courses elegantly served; wines of the finest vintage, women sparkling in riches, satins and jewels less lively than their eyes; men whose glossy expanse of starched shirt front reflected the soft yellow glow of candlelight; a table spread with spotless napery and crowned unto an epergne of wondrous design; at one end the host amiable and truly conscious of his guests; the hostess majestic yet affable at the other end;

a conversation in which both wit and intellect had full play.

Miss Howard found herself seated between Colonel Thornill, a somewhat pompous and emphatic *militaire* with very pronounced views on most things in general and the army in particular, and Mr. Tanturian, F.B.A., whose scientific researches although universally acknowledged to be unfathomable had left him in a state of nebulous doubt as to the significance of any material phenomena whatsoever including his own mortal existence.

'Br-r-r! Yes, by Jove, I shouldn't be surprised if we had 'em over here next year, by Jove!'

'I hold, Miss Howard, that the one thing capable of proof is the non-existence of God.'

'How dreadful! Indeed! But I see Mrs. Brassington is ready to rise,' answered Miss Howard pushing back her chair.

'Oh! My dear young lady!' cried Mr. Tanturian in tones of deep distress. 'What a sad accident! However can it have happened!'

'Why . . . what?' asked Miss Howard anxiously.

'Your pretty gown! Look, some water has been spilled all over it! I hope I haven't upset the finger-bowl inadvertently. No, I see both our bowls are full and there's no stain on the tablecloth. Oh! Dear me!'

'Please, Mr. Tanturian, it's of no consequence,' replied Miss Howard. 'I expect that Lumsden dropped some water when he was filling my glass.'

'But my dear lady, do let me wipe it down with my napkin. I'm afraid your dress is ruined.'

'Not at all—please—I can easily have another breadth put in—excuse me, but I'm keeping Mrs. Brassington waiting,' and Miss Howard quickly followed in the wake of the female train who were slowly defiling from the room.

'Bless my soul, colonel, that young lady, Miss . . . er . . . Miss Howard appears far from well, don't you think so? Very pale and drawn?'

'Hey? Drawn? Who's drawn? Who's discussing pictures anyhow? Br-r-r! Now this question of a foreign invasion . . .'

In August, 1890, there was convened at Leamington a great gathering of savants of all kinds, sorts, countries and qualities. Lectures were to be given in as many tongues as were heard at Pentecost; papers were to be read, *de omnibus rebus et quibusdam aliis*; excurisions were to be made in all directions; meetings were to be held, the stars of either hemisphere were to be exploited, fêted, recreated, applauded, fed, flattered by other constellations; in fact a veritable orgy of intellect and insipidity was arranged. Professor and Mrs. Professor Brassington (who ordered those new bracelets, a new mantle, and two new dresses for the occasion) were not the least of those bidden to take part in this union of the new Deipnosophists.

'Now, Professor, I have been thinking what will be best for Frieda whilst we are at Leamington,' announced Mrs. Brassington.

'Yes, my dear, and you have decided?'

'I have *decided* nothing. It is for you to decide. Have you any better plan to propose than that Frieda and Miss Howard—I have perfect confidence in Miss Howard—should go down to Eastbourne and stay at Mrs. Bibly's? Yes, I know what you are going to say, but we must economise a little. Stop here in that case? No, they can't stop here. I shall be giving the servants their holidays whilst we are away. You never thought of that? Of course you didn't. But I have no time to discuss servants with you now. Do let us keep to the point. With regards to Frieda and Miss Howard, Eastbourne will be a holiday for them both, and where could you get a healthier holiday than by the sea? After all, Mrs. Bibly's, if plain, is quite comfortable, and there's no reason why Frieda shouldn't continue her French and German—I doubt if there's a piano there—but she could go on with the rest of her studies just as if she were at home. I have thought it all out very carefully—I really have to do all the planning in this house—and I do hope, Professor, you aren't going to raise any tiresome objections. Don't you think my suggestion excellent? Frieda and Miss Howard go to Eastbourne the day before we leave for Leamington. And then I can see them off myself. Well now?'

'I quite agree. Admirable. And perhaps you will write to Mrs. Bibly, my dear, and engage the rooms.'

'I have already written to Mrs. Bibly, Professor, and I have taken the rooms for three weeks certain. Do give me some credit for a little forethought. Really, if I hadn't a good head on my shoulders to think and contrive I don't know where you would all be in this house. Yes, Parkins, what is it? Madame La Fleur is upstairs with my new jupon and pelerine? I am coming at once, tell her. You see, Professor, I never have a moment to give to myself, and I am sure I might walk about in rags for all you care. And if at the end of three weeks we want to go north from Leamington to Scarbourgh or Harrogate as may very well be the case, why, Frieda and Miss Howard can stay on at Miss Bibly's, or if she's let they can find other rooms in the town or even move to Worthing or Bognor. So that's settled. And now if I am allowed another five minutes to myself perhaps I may be able to see what Madame La Fleur has done for me. I don't want to disgrace you at Leamington.'

Accordingly, as ordered by authority, one day early in August Miss Howard and Frieda, whose route had been mapped out with the detail and discussion of an Arctic expedition, descended from a four-wheeler at No. 22 Marine Crescent, Eastbourne, and were welcomed by Mrs. Bibly, a voluble little woman, so bent, shrivelled and dried up that she bore a remarkable resemblance to a human button-hook.

'Good morning, my dear, and you'll excuse me calling you so—me knowing you so well and all. Good morning, Miss. Now be careful of that box, cabby, and don't knock it against the wall as you're carrying it up. We don't want any marks here we're better without. There now! If he hasn't been and bumped it against the stair-rails. You be careful, my good man. What? No, I didn't hear what you said and I don't want no sauce. Where's it to go? Why in the back bedroom next to the drawing-room, to be sure. Lor! What a stupe that cabby is! Excuse me, my dear, whilst I go and see he puts it right, and perhaps you'd stop here and bide the door, miss, and mind the coats and umbrellas, in case anyone clips in . . . in a place like this you never know, and full season and all. Right, yes, of course, that's right. Next to the drawing-room, I told you. Didn't know which was the drawing-room? Well, some people have no eyes. What? You say that again. Impertinence! Now, my dear, and you'll pardon me, perhaps you'd better be in the drawing-room—yes, sit down for a minute, do, and keep an eye on the table, you see it's set for lunch. I've got a few new slices of beef and ham in for you, and a loaf and some cheese, and there's butter . . . The other things you will be able to get for yourself this afternoon, and enjoy a little bit o' shopping . . . I like a bit o' shopping meself . . . livens one up I always think . . . and we've got the stores and all so handy . . . Lor! Now I declare I'd been and forgot! If it isn't early closing! Well, I *am* sorry . . . but never mind, we'll manage . . . I shall be only too pleased to lend you an egg or two and a rasher of streaky . . . so that's all right . . . And the cruets are kept in the chiffonier—the door sticks a little but it's quite easy when you are used to it, just give it a sharp pull and oh! my! The knob came right off in me hand! However did that happen? There . . . if I haven't knocked over the salt too . . . Well, spill salt sow sorrow they say . . . What's that? If it isn't that tiresome cabby again! What do you want? Your fare? Well, I never did! You keep an eye on the table, miss, or he may sneak in and have a bit whilst we aren't looking . . . Thank you kindly, and I should think so too! You're far too liberal, miss, that's what it is . . . Carried up the boxes? Well, I should think he did, that's what those fellers are for . . . and now we are all right and straight. You'd like a wash before your dinner? Well, of course, you would . . . I'll have cans of hot water put in your rooms at once! Emma! Emma! Em! Where's that lazy . . . Oh, there you are. Put two cans in the ladies' rooms. And if there's anything else you'd wish for . . . a drop of anything with your dinner . . . I did get some beer in . . . No? Perhaps you'd prefer to have it after, when the young lady's in her room? Or if there's anything else I can easily send Emma round . . . Emma! Emma! Here Em, the lady wants you—what, nothing at all! Well, you do surprise me! Why Mrs. Brassington always . . . And now I'll leave you to have your wash and dinner . . . You'll be hungry travelling . . . And you must tell me what you'd fancy for tea . . . will five-o'clock suit? That's our usual hour . . . and supper, half-past seven. I expect you'll like a cold supper . . . Something hot? Well of course we *can* manage a couple of chops or a steak most nights . . . Yes, to be sure . . . but find it best to have a joint middle-day . . . it eats so well cold at night . . . and these warm evenings people generally want to be out on the pier or what not . . . there's the band and all . . . a pity to stop in . . . you'll find an entertainments list in the hall . . . we lock the front-door at ten sharp. Of course if anyone's going to be later we can always arrange to sit up half-an-hour for them if we get notice . . . we like to know early, and it's only fair we should . . . you've got a lovely view from these windows, as I've no doubt you've already observed . . . Especially from the veranda . . . oh, do just step out on the veranda for a minute . . . it's perfectly safe . . . some sit out on it the whole time they're here . . . and you can see the pier and crowds and all as plain . . . I declare just as if you were down there amongst them . . . and the fireworks on firework nights . . . I ought to charge more for the fireworks . . . of course that's only my joke, miss. But really isn't it a sight? . . . Lovely I call it . . . straight out over the sea . . . The finest view in all Eastbourne, I always say . . . and now what about breakfast? Yes, perhaps you're right, miss, we'd better discuss that after you've had your dinner. And a good appetite I wish you both. We like hearty eaters here. If you want anything more you've only to ring and tell Emma . . . and,' her voice sinking to a confidential whisper, 'if you change your mind, miss . . . well, you understand . . . just give her the money . . . she knows where to get it.'

Eastbourne proved far more enjoyable than Frieda expected. Miss Howard nicely allowed them almost entirely to disregard the Spartan routine prescribed by Mrs. Brassington, so that, save for conversational practice in French, German and Italian, study was temporarily relegated to the background, and a certain amount of lighter reading was permitted. They patronised a local circulating library, whence *Blind Love*, *Kit and Kitty*, and to Frieda's extreme delight *The Romance of Two Worlds* made their appearance unabashed and undisguised.

In spite of her initial disappointment when she realised that no malt liquor and therefore *a fortiori* neither wine nor spirits were drunk by Miss Howard, who in her opinion was very many years younger than a governess had any right to be, Mrs. Bibly in the lower regions of the house confided to her daughter that on the whole she was very well pleased with her visitors' conduct and general behaviour.

'Gentlefolk, that's what they are, Lor, and that's more than one can say of most lets today, and p'r'aps what one wouldn't have expected of a governess, although of course I know missy would be all right. There's no denying they are a bit finicky with their hot suppers three nights a week, and that does give one extra trouble, but we can't have it all the way round as the saying is, and I'm sure I'd rather do a little cooking now and 'gain of an evening than have a parcel of nosey-parkers about the place, who peep and peer and pry here, there and everywhere until one's own kitchen's not safe from them, or else you'll get scrimps who measure the meat by the half-inch and grumble if you give the cat so much as the leaving off their plates or take a crumb of cheese for the mouse-trap. Now that's a ripe bit of Stilton they brought in this morning. You have a taste of it, my dear, for your supper with a biscuit or two, and I'll just cut us a couple of slices off the cold beef first. Bought it at Jobson's they did, so it's sure to be good. Paid a pretty price, I'll be bound. So I think I'll charge them extra for those bedroom candles.'

'All I know, ma,' answered Lou pertly, 'is that the older one—the governess—has some classy frocks. And her handkerchiefs in the draws are lovely stuff too . . . she locks up the wardrobe, the mean thing!'

'Now look here, Lou, and mark my words,' said her mother suspending for a moment her operations on the cold beef, 'don't you go wearing any of her hats or things. You'll get yourself into trouble, my gal. Oh, yes, you will,' in answer to Lou's turns of the head.

'How you do carry on, ma!'

'Well, my dear, you know how nasty that Mrs. Mashham was when she met you on the front . . .'

'Spiteful old cat! Just because I looked better in her blue toque than she did herself. And we thought she'd gone on an excursion as she pretended. Old liar!'

'I'm not saying there was any call for her to be so disagreeable about it, and leave so abruptly when her week was up. But what I do say is—what handkerchief's that, Lou?'

'Never you mind, ma. I'm going to meet Bailey down the prom this evening.'

'Well, you be careful, my girl, that's all I've got to say.'

'Yes, and you be careful with that beef, ma. That's four slices you've cut off already.'

'Well, Emma's got to have her supper, hasn't she? The same as us. And I'm sure we can do with a couple of slices, each. I shall ask her to make it up into a cottage pie for tomorrow night, that's all, with plenty of potatoes. I'll mince it after supper and then no one can't complain. There! Where are the pickles? That's it. Now we're comfortable. Wait a moment! Emma! Em! Here's your supper . . . nice bit o' cold beef and pickles . . . Ah . . . I shouldn't be surprised if the drawing-room were to give you five-a-course when they left, you lucky girl.'

'And I shall have earned it, I shall, an' all,' grumbled Emma clutching her plate with a small show of gratitude.

However can you say so, you lazy thing? Yes, Lor, I'd fancy a glass of beer.'

'Lazy! I like that, mum. It's them front-door steps.'

'Front-door steps? What's wrong with the front-door steps?'

'It's not fair, that's all I've got to say. Giving all this extra work'.

'Extra work?'

'Yes, mum, after I've hearthstoned them and got them as clean as clean—the whole nine of 'em—one of them two comes tramping up and down in wet shoes, mud all over the place, and I've got to do 'em again. 'Tisn't fair.'

'That's funny, Em. Are you sure?'

'Sure? Of course I'm sure, miss. And so anyone would be if they had to do them steps. I don't see where the fuss comes in.'

'But we haven't had any rain these ten days—how could they get wet?'

'I suppose they been out bathing before breakfast. I only know I did them steps at a quarter past eight yesterday morning, d'rectly I'd taken up their tea, and when I looked out about a twenty past nine there they were all messed up as I'm telling you.'

'But if either of those two had been out we'd ha' known it.'

'I can answer for that, ma,' said Lou, who was ready with her cheese, 'neither of them goes out before breakfast.'

'Besides, you took the tea to their room, didn't you, Em?'

'O' course I did.'

'Well, you'd have seen if either of them had been bathing.'

'S'p'ose I should.'

'Isn't that queer now? You go and get your supper, Em. Isn't that queer now, Lou?'

'Lor, ma! How you worry! One of those fellows from the beach selling shrimps, I expect.'

'He'd better not let me catch him mucking up my clean steps,' threatened Mrs. Bibly. 'Why couldn't he have come round the back door? I'll keep a sharp look-out tomorrow, if I have to get up half-an-hour earlier to do it.'

And rise half-an-hour earlier on the morrow Mrs. Bibly—who, good careful soul, spared herself neither time, thought nor trouble where her house was concerned—actually did, but even her gimlet eyes could discover no inconsiderate and slovenly chapman or intruder, whilst the steps after Emma's elbow-grease shone white, untrodden and undefiled.

It was about twelve-o-clock that morning when she was casting up accounts and making mysterious entries in a little book with shiny black covers which was to greet the lodgers on their breakfast-table at the end of the week that Mrs. Bibly was disturbed by the unwanted appearance of Emma at the door.

'Oh, Emma, well, what is it now, when you see I'm so busy? You haven't been and broke anything again? If you have I'll stop it out of your wages, and so I tell you straight—I can't afford——'

'Will you please to come here, mum?' asked Emma grimly leading the way to the upper regions of the hall. 'Tut . . . tut . . . tut . . . oh, I can't have this sort of thing. You were quite right to come and tell me, Emma. I'll go up and speak to them at once,' cried Mrs. Bibly, for her polished parquet oil-cloth was marked by a regular trail of dark muddy footsteps, which crossed the narrow lobby, turned up covering a hall and were clearly defined on the bright Axminster of the stairs. And she ascended, followed by her faithful henchwoman. The footsteps passed the first floor to Miss Howard's bedroom, the second floor front.

'There, Emma, you see. She must have been wearing dreadfully wet and muddy shoes, although how she got them so soaked in this weather unless she has been in the sea is a mystery to me.'

She rapped sharply on the door. No answer. Again she knocked. After a moment's pause she boldly turned the handle and with a preliminary cough entered. 'You'll excuse me, I'm sorry, miss but——' then she stopped short for she was addressing an empty room. 'Well! Oh, she must have come in and out again. That would account for it. I'll speak to her directly after dinner, see if I don't.'

'Begging your pardon mum,' Emma rejoined, 'the two ladies went out just about ten this morning and neither of them has been in since.'

'What! Oh, Emma! Then some man's got into the home! Oh, whatever shall we do? Whatever shall we do?'

'Now, ma, what's the matter with you?' asked Lou, who, bearing a slop-pail in hand, was descending the stairs from her bedroom, gaily carolling:

> 'She'll drive about in a carriage and pair,
> 'With the King on her left-hand side,
> 'And a milk white horse,
> 'As a matter of course,
> 'Whenever she wants to ride . . .
> 'Whenever she wants to ride . . .

'What on earth's the matter?'

'Oh, my dear, there's a man in the house and you singing away there so cold-blooded . . . !'

'Man in the house! Nonsense! I wish there were! There's not been a man in this house since the Millers stayed here from Clapham. After all Frank Miller was fun——'

'Fun! I tell you there's been a strange man in the house, Lou!'

'The grocer's boy stepped inside the back-door or young Percy Wilcox from the dairy with his pint o' cream. Ma, you're making a regular fool of yourself . . .

> 'And a milk white horse,
> 'As a matter of course,
> 'Whenever she wants to ride . . .'

'Making a regular fool of myself, am I? That's a nice way to speak to your mother! Well, then, come and look for yourself, you stupid girl, instead of standing there laughing and singing about milk white horses and such rubbish. See that!' And Mrs. Bibly pointed to the marks with a gesture worthy of Lady Macbeth.

Lou descended and looked. 'See what, ma? I don't see anything.'

Mrs. Bibly gasped. There was not a trace of mud or footsteps on the stair carpet, and when she made her way trembling down to the hall the highly polished oilcloth showed innocent of speck or stain. This was too much. Supported by Lou on one side, and Emma on the other, she sank onto the hard wooden bench stained in imitation of mahogany to match the umbrella stand and exclaimed: 'Well—and Emma can bear me out and all . . . Oh! Oh! Oh!' Symptoms of imminent hysteria appearing, she was somewhat expeditiously hustled down to her own sanctum so that she could give way to her emotions in perfect freedom, undisturbed, but Emma being dispatched to the Red Lion for a quartern of gin her ruffled nerves were eventually soothed by repeated applications of the grateful beverage.

'Oh! Lou! Whatever can it mean?' she asked.

'Never mind, ma. Don't you bother your head about it,' replied her daughter, who evidently had her own ideas of what it meant, although—as she afterwards confided to a friend—'seen ma so put out before, I never have.'

At length Mrs. Bibly was half-persuaded that she had been mistaken, and Emma who showed a strange obstinacy bidden hold her tongue. But the day was not to end without further incident, and Emma was called upon to make a second visit to the neighbouring hostelry, since when Miss Howard, who had gone to her room to take off her hat before their midday dinner, did not appear by a quarter-to-two and Frieda went in search of her it was only to discover the governess lying in a dead faint on the floor. Evidently in falling Miss Howard had knocked over a can or jug in as much as there was a large pool of water spreading over the carpet to the great dismay of Mrs. Bibly who could only be pacified by the promise 'that it should be made good—even if it meant a new rug.'

Upon her recovery from the swoon Miss Howard, who could give no account of her collapse save that she 'felt giddy and stumbled', insisted upon going down to their apartment, where she even made a pretence of eating some lunch. That afternoon she perforce rested on a sofa but absolutely refused to be left alone, almost clinging to Frieda who was anxious to go out to match some wool—a ten-minute job—begging her to defer her errand until the next day when she would accompany her.

Perhaps not very loath, Frieda stuck her needle into the crewel and comfortably settling herself in a cosy chair with the latest book from the library was soon deep in the adventures of the electrical Heliobas and romantic Zarza. Rising, after an hour or so to exchange volume two for volume three, she noticed that Miss Howard had dropped off into a doze although by the clenching of her hands and her half-sighs it would seem that her slumbers brought her anything but refreshment and content. The afternoon was warm, and Frieda crossed the window to open it a little wider to admit the breeze. Apparently the Venetian blinds were swayed a moment in the draught, or else the movement of the window disturbed them for there came a sharp rat-tat as if a person knocking on the pane. Miss Howard jumped to her feet, her face ashy, her eyes distended with terror.

'Gerald! Gerald!' she cried.

'Oh, Miss Howard, I am so sorry,' said Frieda. 'I'm afraid I've awakened you, and I tried to be so quiet!'

'It's nothing—nothing, dear. I must have been dreaming,' answered Miss Howard, sinking back on the couch and passing her hand over her forehead. 'I really thought—it's too stupid—I really thought I saw someone on the veranda tapping at the window.'

'Oh, no, Miss Howard,' replied Frieda, smiling. 'Nobody could possibly climb up on to the veranda.'

'Of course not, dear.'

'You'd better lie down again, Miss Howard.'

'Yes, Frieda. Perhaps I will, at any rate until tea-time. And you?'

'Oh! I have *The Romance of Two Worlds* to finish. You wouldn't like me to read aloud to you?'

'I think not. Thank you very much, my dear, all the same. I'll just doze.'

'How odd! Wherever could that have come from?'

'What is it?' asked Miss Howard, half-opening her eyes.

'Only this funny little bit of gold on the table. It was under my book. I wonder how it got there. It's just like half a coin, only I can't read what's on it. It's foreign. I expect it belongs to Mrs. Bibly or her daughter. I shouldn't be surprised if it were part of a broach, look Miss Howard.'

But Miss Howard had fainted away.

The doctor who was called in—Mrs. Bibly insisted upon that—announced that it was nothing more than a case of overwrought nerves. 'Ah, I only wish I were as sure of that as he seems to be,' observed the good lady to her daughter. 'You mark my words, Lou, she's sickening for something bad—infection, I don't doubt.'

A day or two in bed was prescribed, a complete rest, and a tonic which would be sent round from the chemist almost immediately. 'Have the house full of nurses before we know where we are,' commented Mrs. Bibly. 'I only hope it's nothing inside her like your poor aunt Kezia—her groans were awful. If it's an operation to hospital she'll have to go, for the sight of blood I never could abide—turns me stomach right over. Your cousin Gracie was just the same. She'd throw up her dinner if anyone so much as cut a finger. I mind when your pa had that carbuncle—you were scarcely weaned then so you wouldn't remember, Lou. It was poultices, poultices, poultices. Bread poultices the whole time. And yelling! Oh, he fair yelled when I clapped one on a bit a too hot. Right on the nape of his neck, that was. If there's any night-watching or poulticing a nurse they must have. Not but what old Mrs. Yule'd come in very reasonable I dare say, and she's a respectable old soul.

If there's extra cooking for an invalid there'll have to be extra pay. I've half a mind to write to the young one's ma—what do they call her—Frieda. Pretty name, isn't it? I don't know, Lou, but what I shouldn't be going the best to write to her ma straight away!'

'Oh, you wait, Mrs. Fussbox, and see what the doctor says tomorrow morning? He's coming in, isn't he?'

'Between ten and eleven, my dear. And I wonder what Missy 'll be wanting for her supper tonight. They ordered a rump steak, but it seems silly having that for only one, doesn't it? I thought we might have the steak down here, and I could dish her up some eggs and bacon, or send Em out for a nice chop for her. She won't want to be eating much with her governess in bed and all.'

'If we're going to have the steak, ma, and I won't say as I couldn't relish it, a nice juicy bit o' steak, it'll have to be ready by six-o-clock, because I'm going out this evening.'

'Oh, indeed, miss, and where might you be going to?'

'Sam's taking me to the Devonshire Gardens to see *The Private Secretary* and it starts at eight-fifteen.'

'Private Secretary, indeed! And I'm left here with a house full of sick folk!'

'Don't talk nonsense, ma. There's only the governess in bed.'

'That's not to say there won't be more of us in bed tomorrow. I'm not feeling over well myself. What with these footsteps this morning——'

'Oh, do shut up, ma.'

'Ah, it's all very well to say shut up when you're going gadding out and about with that Sam Bailey and that poor thing lying up there sick in bed.'

'I can't make her well by stopping at home, can I? And if she wants anything isn't there Emma to run up with it for her?'

'Ah, you talk light, my girl, but one day you'll know. Anyhow, if you'd like that bit o' steak at six-o-clock I suppose we'd better have it.'

Whether it was the acting, or whether (as I am more inclined to suppose) it was the escort of Mr. Sam Bailey, there can be no doubt that Miss Bibly immensely enjoyed the futile and facile humours of the Rev. Robert Spaulding, nor was she adverse to a short stroll after the play, so that actually it was close upon midnight when her swain bade her good-bye under the portico of No. 22 Marine Crescent. Lighting the candle which awaited her on the hall-table, she bolted the door, turned out the gas, and took her way upstairs to bed in a merry mood.

'Just fancy him wanting a glass of milk and a Bath bun and not liking London!' she laughed to herself, and then, as she came on to the second landing, she stopped aghast. Outside Miss Howard's door was the figure of a tall man. She did not see the face, since with his back to her he was bending down, and whispering (so she thought) with incredible rapidity through the keyhole. She couldn't distinguish any form of words but in some fashion it was conveyed that he was calling the occupant of the room and bidding her follow him. What seemed so inexplicably horrible, Miss Bibly afterwards said, was that the man was dripping wet from head to foot, his clothes were saturated and sopping, and there was a puffy swollen appearance about the hands which were fumbling at the knob of the door as of one who has lain in the water many days drowned. A second more, and he was no longer to be seen. Whether he had passed into the room or melted into air, she could not tell; later events made her suspect the first.

I do not know what either myself or my readers would have done in such circumstances, but I know what Miss Bibly did—and she appears to me to have been an exceptionally courageous girl.

Looking straight in front of her, and quickening her step without breaking into a run—for that would have been to have given away to abject fear—she walked up to her room, where she locked the door, turned the gas to its full height, and fell breathless into a chair by her bedside. A few minutes later she fancied she heard far below the faint closing of the front door. How she spent that night she cannot remember and she cannot bear to think, only as the room became lighter and lighter with the coming of another sunny August day, she changed her frock, washed her face and hands in cold water, smoothed her hair, and when she heard Emma's familiar tread outside, she went down at 6.30, ready to face the routine of the next four-and-twenty hours.

As may be supposed, her heavy eyes, pale face and somewhat nervous manners did not escape her mother's censure. 'These late hours don't agree with you, my dear, it's plain to see that,' was Mrs. Bibly's remark. 'You're the same as I was. I never could do with the theatre—

that hot and smelly, and one gets crushed up so and scrounged in the pit—always gave me a headache the next day.'

Frieda, as soon as she finished breakfast, was half-minded to go in and see how Miss Howard did, but she agreed to follow Mrs. Bibly's advice, 'I wouldn't disturb her before the doctor's been. Let her have her sleep out.' However, when Dr. Crawford came at ten minutes to eleven, and they entered her room—the door was not locked—there was no patient to be seen. The bed had been slept in. She had evidently risen during the night, dressed herself, and gone out, and that was all.

Miss Bibly kept her own counsel.

It would be superfluous to dwell upon the confusion that ensued, the telegrams that flew to and fro, Emma's hurried journeys to the Crown and Thistle, the incessant conjectures and lamentations and reminiscences of Mrs. Bibly, the interviews with inspectors, the questionings and inquisition. A kindly and considerate man, Dr. Crawford withdrew Frieda from the turmoil and insisted upon her spending the day with his wife, into whose drawing-room a solemn and stately Mrs. Brassington sailed at about eight o'clock that evening. 'It was quite impossible for your father to leave, Frideswide, quite, he has a lecture this afternoon and a dinner with an important soirée to follow tonight, and after all there cannot be the slightest occasion for him to take the journey since *I* am here—at the greatest inconvenience to myself, but of course I am accustomed to *that*. Now, doctor, will you kindly explain to me exactly what has happened.' 'That, madam, I fear is more than any of us can do as yet. The police are making investigations——' 'The police!' 'Yes, madam, it was necessary to call in the aid of the police directly after we found that Miss Howard had disappeared.' 'Disappeared!' 'We can only surmise some obscure nervous lesion, a brainstorm, and that the unfortunate lady rose during the night, and probably altogether unconscious of what she was doing wandered away out of the house.' 'Wandered! Where?'

'Ah, indeed, where?'

The answer to this question was not given until the following day when the body of Miss Howard, fearfully shattered and mangled, was found among the rocks at the base of Beachy Head. She had fallen nearly six hundred feet.

Lectures or no lectures, soirees or no soirees, Professor Brassington was summoned from Leamington at once. The police were so searching and persistent in their question that although she would scarcely admit it even to herself, Mrs. Professor Brassington felt that the situation was getting beyond her.

'The obvious thing to be done, my dear Clara,' said the Professor phlegmatically enough, 'is for you and Frieda to stay at a hotel here, whilst I at once go and interview the only person, who so far as we are aware, may be able to throw any light upon this terrible tragedy—Lady Fitzowen.'

Upon presenting himself at Shanklin Castle a powdered footman informed the astonished caller that Lady Fitzowen was no longer in residence.

'No longer lives here! But surely this is the Fitzowen's seat? Is she dead? Or what?'

'Oh, no, not dead, sir. Perhaps you had better see Mr. Underhill the butler.'

From Mr. Underhill, in a strictly private interview, Professor Brassington learned that shortly after the coming-of-age of Lord Fitzowen, about two years before, the family had let the castle for a long term to a canned meat king from Chicago.

'Things had been going downhill pretty steadily since a good while back, sir, and Lord Fitzowen wasn't the one to pull them together again. He's dead now, sir, died abroad, leaving a widow. It was a sad story.'

'Where is Lady Fitzowen living at present?'

'Well, sir, no disrespect to you, but she leads such a retired life that I am afraid she wouldn't thank me if I were to give you her address. I am sure it's no vulgar curiosity on your part, sir. You must see her? In connection with a death . . . oh, I understand . . . yes, indeed . . . that alters the case certainly . . . she lives not far from here, on the Island, at Garisbrooke . . . her house is next to the Convent. I will write you the full directions on a piece of paper, sir, and may I say I only hope the death is not what I very much fear from the confidence with which you have honoured me it must be.'

An hour or two later found the Professor knocking at the door of a small cottage—it was hardly more— adjoining the Convent of Carmelites at Garisbrooke. He was admitted by a grim taciturn woman of about sixty, who in her spotless cap and apron and black dress had something of the *religieuse* in her appearance, a semblance which was enhanced by her low expression-less voice and silent step. 'You will pardon me, sir, if I leave you in the hall for a moment, I must inquire if my mistress is well enough to see strangers.' She disap-peared, only to re-appear a few seconds after, when she ushered the Professor into a small room plainly and severely furnished, the most prominent object in which was a large crucifix of the realistic Spanish school that hung on one wall. Here was seated an old lady, small and very frail, dressed in deep black and wearing a mantilla. Her hair was white and in her tired eyes was an expression of unutterable sadness. 'Pray be seated, sir, and forgive my discourtesy, in not rising to greet you. I am, as you may see, an invalid,' she said, touch-ing gently a cretel-handled stick of ebony which rested by her side. 'I know your errand, Professor Brassington, before you speak. You are come to tell me that Miss Howard is dead. Is it not so?' 'Unhappily, madam, yes. I presume I see Lady Fitzowen?' 'I am that weary and broken-hearted woman. May I trouble you to touch the bell?' The Professor did so, and quickly the maid entered the room. 'Martha, come here. Kate is dead.' The woman bowed her head without speaking, and passing behind her mistress's chair stood there stern and silent. 'How did she die? Not by her own hand?' 'Oh, no, no, madam. There is no suspicion of that.' 'Thank God! Well, tell me all.'

In a few words the Professor related, softening the thing as much as possible, the recent tragedy. Lady Fitzover signed herself: 'Gerald has killed her.' The maid repeated the sacred gesture. 'Master Gerald has killed her. I always said he would in the end!'

'I will tell you, Professor, all I can, and you must please ask me no more. You may—you almost certainly will upbraid me for my part in the affair, small as it was, I cannot help that. I doubtless deserve your blame, but allow me to say that I should never have given my reference to my poor unhappy daughter-in-law—yes, the lady whom you knew as Miss Howard was Lady Fitzowen, rightfully mistress of Shanklin Castle—unless I had been absolutely certain that both morally and intellectually she was entirely a fit and proper person to educate and have charge of any gentleman's daughter.

'Kate Howard—Howard was her maiden name— had only one fault, and grievous has she been punished for it. She was something of a coquette. Gerald Dunsten had loved her since they were boy and girl together. I do not know that she gave him more encouragement than she did any of the rest who were always dangling after her but he swore a solemn oath that he would marry her and no other man should. I warned her mother once that he was dangerous. Corsican blood flowed in his veins. His father, when quite young, wealthy and utterly irresponsible, during a trip abroad, had married a beauty of Vezzani, a girl of peasant stock, but proud as the oldest families of Rome. I was amazed when I heard that Kate and Gerald were formally engaged. It was too late to plead with her then—Gerald regarded the *sponsalia* as binding as the marriage vow. He made her exchange a broken piece of gold with him—an old custom. I remember her showing it to me with a laugh. And then she met my son, or rather met him after an interval of five years.

'Cyril was within a few months of his twenty-first birthday. They fell passionately—passionately in love. I had never dreamed of anything of the sort, dearly as I would have welcomed her. "Mother," she conferred one evening—her own mother, poor Eva! had died in giving her birth—"Mother, I love Cyril." I expostulated, I begged, I wept, I pointed out to them that she was in honour bound to another man. Words were useless; they were all in all to each other. I urged Kate bravely to tell Gerald even at the eleventh hour, that she did not love him—could not marry him—be the consequences what they might. "I dare not," was her answer, "he would kill me." I trembled. However blind Gerald might be for a while, I knew they could not hope to hoodwink Mariuccia. And she saw. One day I found Kate in tears, and when I asked her what the matter was she told me that Mrs. Dunsten had threatened her horribly if she dared to be false even so much as in thought. Well, things went on smoothly for a time after that. Gerald pressed Kate to name the wedding-day, and after some hesitation she at last consented. He was as happy as the sunshine—and Kate, well I could only hope Kate was resigned. Cyril too, although often silent and *distrait*, had I thought manned himself to accept the inevitable. Perhaps Mariuccia was the only one who realised. Once she remarked to me abruptly: "You know that Gerald and Kate have exchanged the broken pieces of gold? Remind her of it. Gold blessed by the priest and charmed by the sage, binds now and after death. Tell her that." A superstition, it seemed to me, unpleasant and even a little profane. Why should

I frighten the girl? I held my tongue. The wedding morning arrived. The church was thronged, for Gerald Dunsten insisted upon great pomp and ceremony. There was to be a High Nuptial Mass. No bride came to the altar. Cyril and Kate had fled together. They had been secretly married three weeks before. When he knew what had happened—a note from the unhappy girl, all blotched with her tears was brought to the church—Gerald without a tremor in his voice read it aloud before the whole congregation, and with a smile announced: "You will understand, ladies and gentlemen, that it is not my fault there is no marriage this morning. I owe you all my sincerest apology."

'A small half piece of gold fell out of the envelope. Quite calmly he stooped and picking it up put it in his waistcoat pocket to keep company (he said) with the wedding-ring. And then in a flash turning over the tabernacle he cursed her in a stream of foulest blasphemy. Two or three of the men hurried him away at that through the sacristy, biting, scratching and howling like a maniac. I really believe he was not sane. Mariuccia spoke never a word, but her face was that of a devil from the pit.

'. . . Martha, a glass of water . . . No, Professor, let me finish . . . it is my duty . . . Thank you, I am better now . . . That evening Gerald was not to be found . . . I was in an agony . . . I feared lest he had gone in pursuit—and if they met! I had a letter from my son, from Vienna—Kate and he were extravagantly happy— and I wrote at once to put them on their guard. Nearly a fortnight after, Gerald's dead body, horribly battered and torn, was washed up on the shore. He had drowned himself on the evening of his wedding-day. That it was deliberate we cannot doubt, he was an excellent swimmer . . .

'But I knew that could not be the end. Dear as I loved my son and daughter I felt that in some way retribution would fall. And then at the Chantilly races an English milord was shot by a madwoman in the crowd. It was Cyril! Mariuccia had dragged them down. She is now in a *maison de santé* near Versailles.

'Widowed, crushed, utterly forlorn, Kate returned here to me—two hopeless, hapless women! One morning there came a letter addressed to her, a very ordinary looking envelope—the post-mark was London, I remember so perfectly well . . . When she opened it there fell out a half-piece of gold. The letter said: "The day you receive the second half I shall come to fetch you away." It was in Gerald's handwriting. Kate was ill for a long time from the shock. A cruel trick to play? Yes, Gerald was always cruel. When she recovered and could get about again she grew anxious concerning ways and means. She felt that she was a burden on me—of course, my daughter-in-law, Lady Fitzowen, could never be that—we are poor but the family has claims. Nothing would content her, however, save that she must go out into the world and be doing something—some work. For a long time I wouldn't permit it, but at last I gave way. She made up her mind to take a post as a governess. Naturally it was necessary for her to use her maiden name. We talked it over very carefully, and I gave her— well, the reference I wrote to you—please, don't be too angry with me—every word of it is true, and private affairs are private affairs. I am afraid too,' here the voice trembled and dropped a little, 'she dreaded lest by staying here she might involve me in some trouble—yet she was my dear son's wife and I had no fear of Gerald Dunsten—but she used to say to me, "I am convinced, mother, that Gerald will avenge himself. He and his mother swore the vendetta, dead or alive. It is my fault . . . I have brought it on myself, but I will not bring the curse on you . . . I deceived him . . . in my cowardice I deceived him meanly . . . I must dress my wound alone . . . I must suffer . . . and after there may be peace . . ." That peace I pray God poor Kate has found, and may I soon find it too!' and as she bowed her head the old lady's lips moved in prayer.

At the inquest the coroner adopted the view of Dr. Crawford, and an open verdict was returned. I think that Professor Brassington and the former gentleman must have had some private conversation previously, for when the Professor identified the body as that of Lady Fitzowen who had been an inmate of his household as a companion-governess to his daughter, in which capacity she preferred to go under her maiden name of Howard, not much surprise was expressed and no further questions were asked in reference to that point. The coroner indeed observed that the recent and wholly undeserved misfortunes of the Fitzowen family were a matter of public knowledge—which actually was far from the case—and it was highly creditable that the deceased lady when left a widow should ally herself to the noble cause of education, and enter such a family as that of Professor Brassington, no mean name in the roll of our most distinguished scientists.

It is true that whilst the police were searching for anyone who might have encountered the deceased on the night of the accident, there came forward a small shopkeeper who volunteered that he and his wife when returning late on the same day from a summer Cinderella met on the outskirts of Eastborune a tall man with a lady on his arm, walking very quickly, and that this couple seemed to be making in the direction of Beachy Head. But the Inspector didn't appear to think much of this Mr. Groby's story, especially as that gentleman upon being questioned contradicted himself several times and couldn't 'rightly recall', rather conveying the impression that not only lemonade had been in circulation at the 'small and early'. Besides there was no question of any man, tall or short, connected with the case. None-the-less, Mr. Groby, having been thanked with great politeness, left the station feeling a good many inches taller, and over a kipper and a nice cup of tea gave Mrs. Groby a highly-varnished account of the interview, during which he appeared as Sherlock Holmes, Lecoq, and Dr. Thondyke rolled into one. 'Ah! So they don't think that was them?' 'No . . . I don't see how it can be either. And I wouldn't identify them. They were going too fast for that.' 'I don't think you saw them as clear as I did. The fact is that you'd been drinking——' 'Now, Eliza, we've had enough of that. You said you couldn't mention it again.' 'Why, so I did, and I won't. Did you tell them how he was hurrying her along?' 'No . . . I didn't see it, and you've got to be mighty sure with these inspectors.' 'Well, he was, I tell you. Had hold of her arm tight and was making her step out pretty lively. Her face was awful, poor thing! Whoever she was.' 'P'r'aps he was taking off to the doctor's. She may have had a sudden spasm like.' 'Anyhow, Groby, you did right in going along to the station—not that it seems as if you did much good between the lot of you when you got there—but you did quite right to go!'

※

'Ten-o-clock already!' exclaimed my aunt, as her old-fashioned time-piece chimed with its silvery sound like the gentle plash of a fountain in a quiet Italian garden. 'My tale of the governess has taken longer than I thought.'

'Did you know her, aunt?'

'Yes, I knew her, Tony. Don't ask me any more. Poor child, she suffered. But now she's at rest.'

'It seems to me dreadfully unjust——'

'Unjust?'

'That she should have had to go through all that because——'

'Because she sinned, Tony. I knew Gerald Dunstan too. It is a wicked thing to break a man's heart. Yet she loved Cyril . . . Oh! what a tangle the world is! I suppose one day we shall understand it all . . . Get out the bezique cards and markers my dear, I think we have time for a thousand.'

A Toy Theatre

These stage plays are plaguey dangerous things.
—Gay

SOMEBODY once said somewhere that the toys of one generation are the treasures of the next.

This is undeniably true and I suspect it may apply to nothing more aptly than to toy theatres. The robustious old melodramas our fathers, when schoolboys, would present in the Theatre Royal, Back Drawing-room, to an admiring audience of ten or a dozen, *The Brigand, The Maid and the Magpie, Timous the Tartar,* and above all *The Miller and his Men* with the grand finale of a gunpowder (1^d a box) explosion and 'burn blue and red fire' as the curtain fell, are now literally museum pieces, and the sheets of characters—Dangerfelolt, bewhiskered and bristling a cat o' mountain, old Isaac the pedlar with his pack, Masseroni in yellow shirt, red breeches and sugar-loaf hat, and all the rest—repose up and down the Land under the glass cases of our most majestic and Minervan Temple of Culture. There they lie, preserved intact, never to be

98

touched by the nursery scissors, whilst we hoard them, and exhibit them, and lecture on them—frail and precious relics of a bygone age, an age as far away from us as the days of Queen Anne.

Learned books and popular articles alike are written on the Toy Theatre. The art of J.K. Green, of Redington, Skeet, Webb and Pollock is acclaimed. Robert Louis Stevenson is invariably quoted—it is a little difficult to see why.

I am not, however, compiling notes for a history of the 'Penny Plain, Tuppence Coloured'. The thing has already been done. I merely propose to relate an incident which happened in connection with one toy stage, a rather odd affair, which I am very happy to think is not at all likely to take place with regard to any other model.

I have said that the genuinely old Toy Theatres have now become what are commonly called 'Museum Pieces'. You may see one at the Victoria and Albert, South Kensington, for example, and I doubt not they are displayed in all their gorgeous glory at very many other centres of light and education beside.

So much has seemed necessary as a preliminary. I must also explain that the story which has come to me has been transmitted through a diary in the first place—quite an ordinary day by day blotter diary—through some correspondence, and by the courtesy of my friend Jack Ritchie, who knowing I am interested in such things and having had occasion to go pretty carefully through the papers of his uncle Sir Gilbert Ritchie, forwarded to me this bundle with a letter which said, 'since this kind of tale intrigues you, *mon vieux,* make whatever use you like of it.'

Yes, Sir Gilbert Ritchie, F.S.A., of Abbotsleigh, Essex, I mean who died last spring. An authority—perhaps one ought to say *the* authority, in England, at any rate—on Papal coins. But he had a good many other hobbies and side-lines as well, and had got together any amount of jolly stuff of all sorts and kinds. He must have begun to collect tinsel actors, toy theatres, and coloured sheets of characters, for instance, when he was quite a lad, and he certainly kept it up pretty steadily to the end.

It was on a warm afternoon late in April, 1888, according to the Diary, that Sir Gilbert Ritchie found himself in a first-class carriage making his way slowly but agreeably enough through a part of the country, which beside its own very real attraction had the rare charm of being unfamiliar to him. And the occasion of his journey was this. Some eight or nine months before, his friends, the Hunstantons, had bought a house, one of the smaller manor types, at a place called Caeravon—no, that is not quite the right name—but it will be sufficiently located if I say that it is in that part of the country historically known as The Marches, that borderland which seems to have been expressly arranged to create endless trouble for kings and barons in past generations and for small boys in this when it seemed uncertain whether some particular market town might belong to England or to Wales. Sir Gilbert, having been unable to join the Christmas house party had promised for Easter, a season at which he infinitely preferred to pay his visit instead of mingling with a motley merry gathering of uncles and aunts, nephews and nieces, cousins and relations to the nth degree, as many as are listed in the Table of Kindred and Affinity, he would (he was forewarned) find himself one of only three guests, which meant that with any decent luck he might be able well-nigh to monopolise his host upon many an antiquarian excursion, drives and rambles far afield, to all of which he was looking forward with an epicure's anticipation, since Hunstanton was a companion after his own heart in such sharp-set blissful pilgrimages. In fact, our traveller had for some time ceased to follow the Thrilling Adventures of Madame Midas and Gaston Vandeloup, and forgetful of the printed page was gazing with the liveliest pleasure and satisfaction at the passing landscape as the wide panorama lazily spread before him. Yon feudal towers on the slope; those cottages in the dell only marked by the wreaths of blue smoke almost imperceptibly wafted from a score of chimneys into the motionless air; those ivied crumbling walls half-hidden by the trees as the train, stopping wearily at every wayside station, slowly puffed and panted on its toilsome strenuous journey, were all so many unknown mines whence might be dug who knows what treasures, what gems of antiquity?

A true gourmet, Sir Gilbert, was already—metaphorically—licking his lips and sniffing the bouquet of ruined priories and castles unexplored.

Indeed, presently his eyes, perhaps like those of Mr. Pickwick on a famous occasion, closed as with excess of pleasure—it was a distinctly warm afternoon—and he was undisguisedly somnolent when, as the shadows were already beginning to lengthen, the long journey ended at five twenty-seven, and he was roused by a sharp brisk tread on the platform pier and the wide opening of his carriage door. Even before he was well out of his seat he found his hand warmly grasped by Tom Hunstanton whose cheery voice sounded: 'Aha! You've a miracle, Ritchie! Why the train is actually to time for once! Here! Where are your traps? A portmanteau in the van? Right! Davies, you see to that! What, the gentleman's ticket!' to a smiling country porter who was touching his cap expectantly, 'Oh! Of course. We'll just spank along in the dog-cart. I thought you'd like it better than the brougham which Ella wanted me to send. Leave your handbag to come along with the portmanteau, that is unless there's anything you need from it at once. No? Good then. It'll be up in less than half-an-hour after we are. Right away! Give her her head!' and as the mare started off in full fettle the little tiger nimbly nipped up behind.

In a few minutes they had passed through the main street of the old town and were gaining the open country. 'Upon my word, I must say you've chosen a remarkably pleasant part of the world,' commented Ritchie, looking about him 'in mighty content'—so old Pepys has it—whilst they sped through the freshly scented lanes, 'remarkably pleasant, and interesting too if I am not mistaken.' 'Yes, we all of us like it, and we are shaking down splendidly. I don't say that the wife isn't looking forward to a month or two in Town later on,' replied Hunstanton, flicking the mare meditatively between the ears with his whip, 'and so am I as well for the matter of that. And when the time comes round we shall be equally looking forward to getting back home again.'

'Well, that's as it should be. And now, tell me, have you been doing much writing lately? What about that article on George Ripley and his *Twelve Gates* you started on? That will be valuable. Did you make anything of it?'

Even if the Manor had been less attractive than it was both inside and out Sir Gilbert Ritchie was prepared to be thoroughly appreciative, so that whilst they sat over a late tea-table in the oak-beamed hall his commendations of the long low house with the mullioned windows set deeply in the thick grey wall won his hostess's heart from their very sincerity and intelligence of understanding.

'I am so glad you really like the Manor, Sir Gilbert. You hardly know how much I have been looking forward to you coming here and seeing it. I was disappointed about Christmas . . . yes, of course it is much more agreeable out of doors and easier getting about now . . . yet we had such a nice party at Christmas.'

'I am sure you did, Mrs. Hunstanton. But the Manor couldn't be more charming that it is this minute.'

'Do you honestly think so? Well, I *am* glad. Because . . . yes, I will confess it . . . do you know I've been just a wee bit afraid about you coming too!'

'Afraid! My dear lady, am I such a terrible person? I declare it is you who are beginning to make me feel distinctly nervous.'

'Oh, no . . . I didn't mean that at all. Only you are so critical and such an authority. And I've started to love the Manor, I really have.'

'I am not surprised to hear it.'

'How nice of you to say so! Well, I was quite anxious, Sir Gilbert, lest you should find something wrong, something second-rate about it.'

'You need not be afraid of that. It is a charming place. I envy you immensely.'

'You make me feel very proud. Indeed you do.'

'Sincerely you are to be congratulated. No, no more tea, thanks. I've had my second cup already.'

'Oh! But you must, after your journey. These are such tiny cups too. I am sure you are dreadfully hungry and tired.'

'Hardly hungry. A trifle tired, perhaps, and thirsty, I acknowledge.'

'Well then . . .'

'By the way,' broke in Hunstanton, who was beginning to get a little impatient of small-talk and social stichomythia, 'tomorrow I've arranged that in the morning we drive over to Wrythen and see the Abbey—Cistercian, you know—and then I thought we might lunch at Northop, it's only a little further on, and in the afternoon on our way back take in Llanaeron—there's a fine old church there—and——'

'Oh! Tom!' rebuked his wife, 'what an excursion! Fancy dragging Sir Gilbert out all that way directly after he arrives! It's miles! Do give him time to rest and settle down first. Why, he hasn't even finished his tea after hours in the train—you know what those trains are!—and already you are talking about going over to Wrythen. It's a long drive, Sir Gilbert, and very tiring. At least I generally find it so. Oh! I won't say it isn't worth it when you get there. The ruins are magnificent, but very lonely and just a bit frightening I think.'

'But, Ella, Gilbert is very keen on seeing Wrythen. Aren't you Gilbert?'

'So he may be, Tom, but don't hurry him. You are always in such a hurry. Do let us take things quietly. If Gilbert is wise he will go and have a nap after his journey. He'll have time to get in a good hour before the dressing-bell. And I've asked the Vicar and his wife and Miss Maitland in for whist after dinner, so that with Kitty and Colonel Duncombe we shall be able to make up two tables. We shall want you to play tonight, Tom. Are you fond of whist, Sir Gilbert?'

It cannot be denied that Tom's florid face fell perceptibly when he heard of the evening's engagements, and he could not refrain from a wry grimace at his guest, a spasm which owing to a deft use of the handkerchief and a loud trumpeting of the nose happily passed unseen by his wife. Sir Gilbert, too, felt a trifle damped, since he had been anticipating a long hob-nob in the most private recesses of his host's sanctum sanctorum. But he hid his emotions with a gallant effort, and so far succeeded in declaring his delight in cards with such glowing encomia as enshrined him forever in his hostess's favour as 'a really useful man.'

Mrs. Hunstanton rang the bell. 'Show Sir Gilbert to his room, Jenner,' she directed as the butler appeared at the door. 'Have you unpacked his bag?'

'It has only just come, ma'am, and I was going to ask the gentleman for his keys.'

'Only just come! Why couldn't it come up with you in the brougham? . . . Oh! Tom! You didn't take the dog-cart to the station after all I said! You know what those porters are! Why the luggage might have been left out on the platform all night, and I can't think what we should have done.'

'No, my dear, nothing so tragic would have taken place, for we should have sent for it. After all, it's never happened like that here.'

'How can you say so, Tom, when you know how Miss Murdoch was treated?'

'Nonsense, my dear, it was only her umbrella she left behind, and it turned out that she had left it in the railway carriage.'

'Umbrella or not, I know that she was quite cross about it, and you go on as though your guests' luggage was of no consequence at all. People who come here will think we are perfect-savages. I declare you are getting worse and worse. You care for nothing but your old stones and books and priories and what not. Yes, it's all very well, dear, but consider how uncomfortable Sir Gilbert would have been without a stitch and——'

'Anyhow, his things are here now safe and sound, and that's all about it.'

'I really do believe Tom gets worse every day, Sir Gilbert.'

'Oh! He was always pretty bad,' smiled his friend.

'And I am so sorry about your luggage.'

'I am sure that's quite all right, thank you.'

106

'Only suppose you had wanted something straight away!'

'Well, you see, he didn't, Ella,' interposed Hunstanton with some warmth.

'Anyhow it ought to have come up with you. I shall see myself that the brougham goes to the station another time,' rejoined his wife, determined that hers should be the final word.

The evening passed pleasantly enough. The Vicar was a scholar of parts with a fund of anecdotes much of which were really humorous and witty, whilst his wife showed herself no lukewarm nor inexpert advocate of the card-table, and at a quarter past eleven Sir Gilbert as her partner rose from his chair having won a hard-fought rubber under such conditions as Mdm. Battle herself would not have disdained.

The next morning, not without much admonitory counsel from Mrs. Hunstanton, the proposed excursion to Wrythen Abbey took place, and an excellent lunch was eaten at the King's Head, Northop, a house renowned for its humming home-brew, which indeed constitutes the chief (I might say the only) attraction of the place, since truth be told otherwise it is a very ordinary and rather unprepossessing backwash of a town. St. David's, Llamaeron, afforded a rare treat. There is the old tooth ornament in the porch, a Christopher who can be clearly discerned under the plaster, a piscina and a font which are almost undamaged, and some good glass over the altar. In fact, the two friends reached home not a little late for dinner—an accident for which Mrs. Hunstanton from her experience of similar jaunts had wisely made provision—but they were full of discussion and supremely happy.

Although the entire neighbourhood proved delightfully interesting, far more interesting (as the Diary leaves ample evidence) than Sir Gilbert Ritchie could have guessed, naturally every day was not allowed to be devoted to such congenial explorations. On Sunday, for example, as at Northanger, the whole time between morning and evening service was spent in exercise abroad or eating cold meat at home. The social duties of his hostess, too, had certain claims, which she was magnanimous enough not to press unseasonably, but which notwithstanding must in measure be satisfied. She was indeed so far in advance of her period that she did not piece and parcel out every minute of her guest's day betwixt breakfast and bed, cyclonically descending upon him whilst he was in the thorough enjoyment of a quiet morning in the garden with his pipe and a book, and volubly insisting that he must be bored with the place, 'the sameness of every day's society and employments.' Perhaps it was upon a hint or rather more than a hint from Hunstanton himself that he was left so very much to follow his own devices, a dispensation for which he is unsparing in his private expressions of gratitude and acknowledgement. Unless there chanced to be the serious business of an all-day outing on hand, lawn tennis or croquet could not ordinarily be shirked in the afternoon, but after dinner again no sooner were the coffee cups emptied then both host and guest were wont to disappear from the drawing-room and rid the ladies of their presence with the most unconventional celerity, whilst the confabs in the study lasted late and long.

In return, moreover, for his chivalrous service at the ritual of the five-o-clock tea-table it was generally understood that until lunch-time must be considered Sir Gilbert Ritchie's own, and it was on one of these occasions that he met with—or rather opened the door for—the adventure which led to this tale.

During the middle of the morning,—it happened on the last morning of his visit, for he was leaving next day—when the sunshine outside was especially bright and tempting, having written some letters to Germany and finding himself in need of a few twopenny-halfpenny stamps, rather than trouble his hosts by asking in the house he resolved to stroll down forthwith to Caeravon post-office, not being at all sorry in fact to find an errand which would afford him both incentive and excuse for a very pleasant walk of half an hour to and from the old town, among whose quaint streets he was never loath to loiter and look about him.

His purchase completed, a few words on the weather exchanged with the good gossip who presided over the local distribution of Her Majesty's Mail, his letter duly dispatched to Leipzig, München, and Nona, he felt at liberty to saunter awhile, and soon found himself rather aimlessly wandering down a narrow street, or rather lane, winding round at the back of the market, which he did not remember having noticed before. There were a few shops of the smaller kind, and these grew more heterogeneous and humbler, albeit none the less interesting for that, as one left the square and its stalls further behind. Here were bow-shaped windows, thick-paned and divided like a chequer-board, a couple of centuries old.

In one of the shabbiest and dustier of these, amid the miscellanea, soap, candles, flannel, mops, cheap jubilee mugs of the previous year, chipped cruets, odd cups and saucers, derelict volumes of gaunt and forbidding appearance, blatant oleographs, glass paper weights, envelopes exhibiting local views, and an altogether endless jumblement beside, their lurked a maple-framed tinsel picture of some absurd actor at Astley's of the Grecian Salon in the role of Aureato, the Golden Knight. This, although no great thing in itself, was at least sufficiently attractive to invite a closer inspection, and if a very reasonable price asked, perhaps even to purchase.

To the loud clanging of an ancient bell Sir Gilbert pushed open the door and stumbling down one step rather abruptly entered the dark and dingy little den. At the noise there appeared from an inner room, screened off by a heavy plush curtain, a little fat old woman in a rusty black gown with a cap of tangled black net on her thinning grey curls. A knitted shawl whose garish blues and yellows age and dirt had long since successfully achromatised was clasped over her ample and panting bosom by a huge cameo brooch to which she pressed her mittened hands whilst she wheezed and peered uncertainly through her silver spectacles. As though to sharpen her wits she drew a tin-box from her apron pocket and regaled herself with a pinch of snuff, with which indeed both her gown and upper lip were already plentifully bestowed, nor could her interlocutor fail to remark the slight but significant odour of gin that accompanied her nearer advance. Her flabby wrinkled faced seemed to express surprise at a customer, especially so well-dressed and distinguished looking a gentleman, but with a truly genteel half-curtsey she politely enough inquired what he wanted.

It was not without some difficulty, the knocking over of a couple of bars of soap which looked exactly like marble in its colour and consistency and the scattering in all directions of a box of night-lights to the accompaniment of a good deal of tut-tutting and puffing, that the Golden Knight was retrieved from his obscure and forgotten corner in the window, but the labour proved worthwhile in the end, for when his glass had been somewhat unceremoniously dusted by the lady's apron and he was examined near at hand he turned out to be an early impression of this heroic and romantically handsome chevalier, whose sumptuous armour literally dazzled with the sheen of a thousand spangles.

The price asked was small, and as the lady proceeded in rather bat-like fashion to institute a search for a stray piece of paper wherein to wrap up the purchase, Sir Gilbert, highly delighted with himself and emboldened by so unexpected a pennyworth, asked whether there were not any more similar prints or pictures lurking in the recesses of her shop.

To answer the question involved a complete cessation of the business upon which she was engaged, a prolonged pinch of snuff followed by folding of the hands on the most prominent and protuberant part of her person, a closing of the eyes and a gentle swaying the head from side to side as a symbol of polite negation.

'No, sir, I'm afraid not . . . nothing that I can call to mind . . .' and then after a further moment of deep reflection, 'no, not one. Nothing of the sort.'

'Ah!' replied Sir Gilbert, dryly, for he instinctively felt that had he demanded candles or soap or a mop or even one of those indefensible pannikins which dangled under his very nose the answer would have been precisely the same.

'Nothing of the sort,' chanted the presiding priestess, who had at last discovered a sheet of crumpled newspaper in which she was enfolding the picture.

'Well, then, I'm afraid that's all . . .'

'Yes, sir; thank you, sir.'

'One moment though! What's that over there?'

'Where? On the second shelf? Oh, yes, I recollect that a picture . . . so it is . . . Reach it down? Certainly sir. Pouf! Pouf! It's me breath comes so short these days. It's not worth bothering with the steps, and I don't know where they are, that's a fact. It's not often I'm wanted to touch the things on this shelf. Eh! Some of them have lain there years. If I just stand on this little box I can manage it. Pouf! Pouf! Dusty? Why, yes, it is a bit dusty. Just let me give a rub over. A framed picture, and I declare just like the other! But I can't see the name. Perhaps you can read it, sir, your eyes will be better than mine, and there's no denying it's a bit dark in here.'

'Mr. Romantzini as Zanga,' read aloud Sir Gilbert. And then to himself: 'You splendid fellows!'

'It's me memory that's so bad these days.'

'And what do you want for this?'

'Well, sir, since it's just the same as the other, a pair one might say, I suppose it'll be the same price. Shall I wrap 'em up together? Thank you, sir. Mr. Romantzini as Zanga, did you say? Me hearings not as good as it was.'

'Yes'

'I recollect him well. Eh! That's him right enough,' as she peered at the print. 'And I've seen the play too, although the name of it I can't for the life of me remember, not if anyone was to offer me hundreds.'

'You remember him? I don't think I ever heard his name before.'

'Lor! Only fancy that, sir! Oh, he was a very great actor, and very well-known he was in his time . . . very well-known. But that must be close on five-and-forty years ago now. Yes, it's all that. My poor husband—he's been dead and gone these nineteen years come Bartlemas—my poor husband was Mr. Romantzini's dresser at the Adelaide, and he admired him very much. Oh, yes, there's no doubt about that. My Zekiel admired Mr. Romantzini very much. Many a story he could tell about the theatre and their goings-on, many a story. I only wish I had a shilling for every time he's told me of Mr. Romantzini.'

'That's interesting. Your husband an actor's dresser. Then I suppose these pictures were his?'

'Yes, sir. He had a number of them. I've got a good few put away somewhere at the back now. But I shan't ever sell those. Not that I'm so rare fond of them as he used to be. 'Twas after he died I took half-a-dozen maybe from the bedroom, and put 'em in the shop. I don't care for them on my walls, and that's the plain truth. I'd rather see a nice text or two, they're more comfortable and cheerful like. Besides, I'm a chapel-woman now, and I don't hold any longer with these things, whether I did once. Not that my Zekiel wasn't a good man too . . . for he was. After we left Lunnon way back, and came here he turned over quite a new leaf. Chapel reg'lar and a stout one for the Bible and prayer meetings he was. Oh, Zekiel Morgan was a warm man for religion. I wasn't converted til we'd been here a long while. Mrs. Morgan, I am. You may have noticed the name over the shop. This was Zekiel's own town. Ay, he was from here, he was, that's why we came here all the way from Lunnon.'

'Well, look here, Mrs. Morgan—ma'am—are you sure you haven't got anything more in this line . . . anything else belonging to your husband, say, that you are willing to get rid of?'

'No, sir, nothing that I can recall just . . . I'm not denying me memory's that bad . . . Should I come across anything I'll put it by.'

'But I am leaving here tomorrow.'

'Ah! That's a pity now.'

'You say your husband was a dresser?'

'He was. Dresser to Mr. Romantzini. And rare proud of it he was too!'

'Didn't he have any old props, suits, actors stuff, anything of that kind?'

114

'Lor bless you, sir, no! We sold all the wardrobe before we left Lunnon. Mr. Romantzini gave him a lot o' things from time to time. The Bower—that was down Lambeth way, bought them all off from him.'

'You're quite sure then you've nothing left at all?' came a last insistent appeal.

'No . . . I don't think so . . . I can't recollect . . . yet wait a minute. Perhaps this would be in your line, sir?' And shuffling round the counter to an old chiffonier stowed away at the back of the shop, Mrs. Morgan threw aside a piece of tattered red baize which covered a large square object that stood on the top, and Sir Gilbert knew that he had come across something good.

It was a Toy Theatre. Rather larger than the ordinary size stage of the juvenile drama—actually it spanned some twenty-four inches by eighteen as he measured it afterwards—the model was more perfectly fitted than any he had previously seen. There was the elaborately 'built up' stage front in the massive classical style, beyond which projected the apron furnished with its rows of five footlights naked and unashamed. Across the top of the proscenium arch—itself surmounted by a conventional bust of Shakespeare—stretched a garish panel depicting Apollo, lyre in hand, clad in a tunic of vermillion and Prussian blue, who was driving a Roman chariot through thick feathered clouds amid a burst of radiant sunshine whilst Victorian nymphs seemly garmented in gamboge, magenta and emerald, gambolled and hovered with their fairy wings about his triumphant car. Three smaller panels below severally presented a Gothic tournament, Mazeppa on his horse, and a woodland of strange vegetation where brigands caroused. There were four boxes crammed with an elegant audience of rakes and belles attired after the fashion of William IV, all of whom seemed to be intensely occupied in directing their fixed and stony gaze anywhere save at the stage. A similar characteristic marked the musicians on the 'orchestra strip', who, notwithstanding their instruments raised in full blast, turned their backs with the completest indifference to their leader, who, kit in one hand, seemed to be wielding his baton with unprecedented gusto and vigour. Below the boxes showed the proscenium doors, each duly fitted with brass-door-knobs and knockers. Gas lamps with opaque shades were clustered on either side. There was the scarlet curtain with heavy gold fringe—impractical—but behind was lowered the traditional green glazed calico curtain. It was a splendid Toy Theatre—and it was something more.

Sir Gilbert looked at it in silence, enraptured. The old woman stood without speaking at his side.

It would not do, however, to be too laudatory, too enthusiastic, and so after a minute he remarked in an elaborately casual voice: 'Yes, it's a nice piece enough.' Then the collector breaking through: 'Has it a pedigree? I mean do you know who made it? West perhaps, or Hodgson, or Marks?'

'I don't know anything about any pedigree,' ruminated the old lady, 'and I never heard of West or Marks, and what was the other name? But my husband made that theatre with his own hands, ay, made it himself he did, he was a rare handy one to do a bit of carpentering about the house, that I will say, I do miss him for that. Yes, to be sure, Zekiel made that, and I kept it lying by me so long that I declare I'd clean forgotten it.'

'It's a good bit larger than most of them, I think, and that makes a little awkward,' quoth Sir Gilbert with a side-glance at Mrs. Morgan to see if would rise to the bait. An inexpressive and entirely uninterested 'Lor now! Is it then?' was her only rejoinder.

He tried another tack. 'Are there any sheets of characters or scenes?'

'Not that I know of . . . I don't mind that there were ever any characters.'

'Oh! Well . . . Can I raise the curtain at any rate, and look at the stage?'

'Lor bless me! Yes, please, sir. I suppose it works at the side—hereabouts—but me old fingers are getting crippled now, sadly crippled . . . that but once they were quick and busy enough . . . a great needle woman, I was, and needed to be . . . What with a husband and his cravats to make and shirts and vests and pants to patch and darn . . . ah! There it goes!' and after Mrs. Morgan had fumbled for a minute or two at the side of the proscenium the green glazed calico curtain slowed rolled up and revealed to Sir Gilbert a miniature set scene.

It was so realistically done that for a moment he was startled. It seemed as if the curtain had gone up on an actual stage. The set was a bedroom, a bedroom of 1835 in fact. A fantastically designed black-cloth showed a gay wall-paper with a pattern of huge blowsy flowers. There was a dressing-table swathed in spotted white muslin, a vast and cumbrous wardrobe, a tabouret, a cheval glass. On the six wings, innocent of perspective, was painted two or three stiffly ranged chairs and a couple of pictures in heavily-moulded gilt frames. The time was evidently night, since the curtains 'in many a fold and vast', draped upon a mahogany pole huge as Goliath's spear, was closely drawn over the windows, and on the dressing-table was set a very ordinary chamber candlestick with snuffers complete in which burned a tall wax taper.

Two characters held the stage. One was a woman represented as asleep in a huge four-poster bed. In spite of the crude colouring somehow she made a striking and even beautiful figure. The fair hair hung down in ringlets over the pillow, and the artist—for he *must* have been an artist of no mean quality—had given her a face of virginal innocence and purity. The other actor was an even more arresting figure. A tall man of magnificent proportions, ebon black, wearing on his head a Madras muslin turban broached with a large brass crescent, with billowy Turkish trousers of white batiste, yellow slippers, red stockings, a crimson satin garandine emblazoned with gems and gold to rival the glitter of a Bond Street jeweller's window, the whole girt by a sea-green sash into which was stuck a mighty scimitar. He stood there, menacing, terrific, as he gazed down upon the sleeping girl, and however crude the colours and rough the execution so marvellous had the figures been drawn and so neatly cut out that for a moment they almost to be alive, mere puny painted bits of pasteboard that they were!

118

Sir Gilbert started: 'Why, of course. Othello!'

He stopped short and sharp. Had he by so un-guarded an exclamation given the old lady a clue to the rarity—possibility the unique rarity—of her husband's handiwork? But no, Mrs. Morgan who was solac-ing herself with a prolonged pinch of snuff appeared sublimely indifferent whether the drama displayed was *Othello* or *The Red Rover* or *Jane, the Licensed Victualler's Daughter*. In fact she would probably have been more interested in the latter piece.

A brief parley secured the Toy Theatre for Sir Gilbert at a figure something less than moderate. The only difficulty was how to convey his new purchase home, for in the true spirit of the genuine enthusiast he was resolved that it must accompany him there and then. On being appealed to Mrs. Morgan herself nota-bly failed to rise to the occasion, and after much snuff and rheumy cogitation could only deliver herself of the hesitant statement that Owen Price a jobbing gardener in the next street 'had a barrow' he was want to em-ploy for the conveyance of plants, and which he might loan but she couldn't be sure, although he was most certainly out at work—she didn't rightly know where, maybe at Miss Morris' or maybe at the vicarage—and as perhaps the barrow was *hors de combat*—she seemed to remember it had lost a wheel—there was in the end little profit gained from her suggestion.

The situation was finally met by the hiring of a fly from the 'Red Lion'. This proved to be a roomy and somewhat antiquated vehicle, smelling suspiciously enough of damp and long disuse, whose passage and solemn halt before Mrs. Morgan's shop at once drew a number of curious gazers to their doors, and afforded a lively subject of rumour and speculation, the tender youth of the neighbourhood who collected in great and grubby force being roused to demonstration of an almost unprecedented excitement when assisted by the local Jehu Sir Gilbert carefully committed a large and mysterious package to the recesses of the cab.

Not a few of the more active and inquisitive larrikins indeed tried to keep pace with the horse as it moved slowly away, and Sir Gilbert felt some relief when with many uncouth abjurations from the box and indiscriminate slashing of the whip to the right and left they outdistanced their ragged escort.

But the arrival at the Manor was not to be achieved without some bustle, since the luncheon gong having boomed forth its clarion summons ten minutes before and Sir Gilbert not having appeared with his wonted punctuality Mrs. Hunstanton who espied and recognised from the dining-room window the 'Red Lion' fly at once jumped to the conclusion her guest had met with an accident which compelled him to be driven back from his walk.

His apologies were received with a good grace but there was subtle undercurrent of reproof meanwhile and his hostess made it understood gently that a Toy Theatre was by no means an adequate reason to excuse one for being late for lunch.

'A Toy Theatre! What an extraordinary idea! I beg your pardon Sir Gilbert, but it *is*, isn't it? I suppose you bought it for one of your little nephews or nieces? That huge thing! Oh! Sir Gilbert you really shouldn't have dragged it all the way from town. I am sure you must be tired out. It's no use saying you're not. I know you are. We could so easily have sent down for it this afternoon too. Davis is calling at the station for a couple of important parcels I am expecting from London by the four-o-clock train, and it would have been no trouble at all.'

'I am so sorry to be late for lunch, Mrs. Hunstanton. You must forgive me, I had only intended to walk down to the post-office and back, and then I got glancing in one of two of the old shop-windows and the time simply flew.'

'Oh! It doesn't matter about lunch at all. It's you I was thinking about. I was so anxious. I know there are all sorts of odd places in Caeravon. Very dirty most of them look to me too, but there! You men never mind anything about that. But what really worries me is how you must have been jolted about in the horrid ramshackle old cab! I wonder you ever got back at all alive! I really do! Now I am sure you want a good wash after it. And you must be terribly hungry—oh, no, it's no use saying you're not, after walking all that long way—and here I am keeping you talking—oh! How thoughtless of me!'

'I shan't be five minutes, Mrs. Hunstanton, Just a wash and a brush!'

'Oh! Don't attempt to carry that huge parcel yourself! It's bound to be fearfully heavy.'

'No, indeed, it's quite light, only perhaps a wee bit awkward.'

'Awkward! Of course it is. Would you like it upstairs at once? Yes? Now you can't manage it. I know how you men are with these things. I am sure Tom—oh, Jenner, see this is taken up to Sir Gilbert's room, please. Yes, now, at once.'

'Yes, ma'am.'

'You'll be careful, won't you, Jenner?' admonished Sir Gilbert as he began to mount the stairs. 'It's fragile and rather valuable.'

'Then perhaps I'd better fetch Lucy to help me carry, ma'am?'

'Oh, yes, Jenner, if it's anything breakable.'

'Thank you, ma'am. I assure you, sir'—with a formal starched bow to the disappearing Sir Gilbert—'every precaution shall be taken. You may entirely rely on us. We are accustomed to handling this sort of thing for the master.'

In order to atone for his offence of the morning, and seeing that it was the eve of his departure from the Manor, Sir Gilbert felt it incumbent upon him to throw himself absolutely at his hostess's beck and call *en cavaliere servante* throughout the rest of the day, and since—not to mention Sunday odd callers—a party of chaperons, maidens fair and their beaux, two wagon-ettes full drove in for the lawn tennis and croquet soon after lunch, which domestic sports were followed by a small and early carpet-dance, it was not until close upon midnight, and then only by pleading his next day's journey, that Sir Gilbert was permitted to repair to the bed for which he yawned and yearned a couple of hours ago. As we might suppose, the first thing he did was to turn to the Toy Theatre which had been arranged by the considerate Jenners upon a large table in the bay directly opposite of the front of his bed. Even his new purchase did not detain him long—he promised himself a fuller and more delightful inspection at home tomorrow—so after one or two minutes of rapturous anticipation, he laid himself between the sheets in a highly complacent and self-congratulatory frame of mind.

Sleep was only a few minutes in coming, and he had no idea how long could have elapsed before he was startled out of a very placid and refreshing slumber by a strain of music.

The first thought that flashed across his mind was that the dance downstairs must be continuing into the small hours. Yet that seemed impossible. His bedroom lay far away from the main portion of the house, in a wing at the end of a corridor where no sounds save the loudest would have reached. Besides, all but some half-a-dozen dauntless couples had taken their leave before he withdrew to rest.

The strain was repeated and increased in volume, brassy and sonorous as though a whole orchestra were in full swing. He was so much startled that he suddenly sat up in bed, and became conscious in some curious way that he was no longer alone in his own room, but made one in a crowded building of some sort with people all about him. He seemed to be in a small loge; in front of him was a velvet-padded balcony on which lay a printed slip of paper and—yes—a pair of opera-glasses; musty dank curtains were draped on either side and valanced above.

The music sounded louder. From below there rose an indiscriminate hum of voices as if of a numerous assembly.

He looked out . . . in the half-light he was aware of a vast auditorium, full of figures, shadowy and ill-defined . . . people seemed to be moving to and fro . . . there stretched a huge gilt proscenium of heavy Corinthian design that framed an expanse of dull green cloth. The atmosphere was hot and breathless with the smell of cheap scent, sweating humanity, gas and orange-peel.

Mechanically he took up the paper which before him—it was vilely printed—and read:

OTHELLO . . . Mr. ROMANTZINI
DESDEMONA . . . Miss LANGRIVIER
Iago . . . Mr. Delamare
Cassio . . .

'I'm intended to see something,' he thought as it fluttered from his nervous hand. 'What?'

A crescendo . . . the music abruptly ceased . . . he could hear odd rustlings, hawks and hems, half-stifled coughs.

The curtain rose. The scene was a bedroom. There was a conventional back-cloth, the wall-paper pat-terned with huge blowsy flowers. There was a dressing-table swathed in spotted white muslin, a vast wardrobe whose amber glass knobs reflected a glint of light, a tabouret, a cheval-glass. In a large four-poster bed the curtains of which were drawn apart lay a young and beautiful girl, some eighteen years old. Her golden hair streamed down over the pillow. Her eyes are closed, her hands lightly clasped as if in slumber.

A door at the back opened. There entered a tall man, ebon black, wearing on his head an ample white turban broached with a brass crescent. His attire was gorgeous, yellow slippers, red stockings, a crimson satin robe glittering with gold and gems, encircled by a sea-green sash. In his hand he carried a candlestick with a lighted taper which he set down on the dressing-table before he stalked forward and stood by the foot of the bed.

Sir Gilbert could see that the actor was under the influence of some terrific emotion. His long sinewy fingers clenched and unclenched themselves in the folds of his gown. He seemed trembling from head to foot.

> It is the cause, it is the cause, my soul;
> Let me not name it to you, you chaste stars!
> It is the cause. Yet I'll not shed her blood . . .

His magnificent voice, throbbing with agony, pierced through the house. What an actor the man was! Sir Gilbert caught his breath as he gazed and listened, fearful of all beside . . . The girl in the bed stirred, opened her eyes:

> Who's there? Othello?
> Ay, Desdemona.

As the dialogue proceeded, a growing horror chilled Sir Gilbert. His scalp prickled and twitched with cold animal fear; his skin rose in goose-flesh. He felt he must shuffle to his feet . . . this must not go on . . . it must be interrupted at all costs before the catastrophe came. And yet he remained spell-bound; unable to stir hand or foot; unable to articulate, his mouth parched and dry; shuddering in his place.

'Sweet soul, take heed, take heed of perjury;

'Thou art on thy death-bed.'

'Ay, but not yet to die.'

'Presently . . .'

Oh! Would no one stop it? Would it never stop? Couldn't they see? This was no acting.

The man's eyes were blazing red with fury; his teeth gnashed and grinned; the foam literally dripped from his slavering lips. He stood at the bedside like some gigantic figure of incarnate evil.

The girl rose frightened as she looked at him, struggled to her knees, and uttered a stifled cry.

'Down, strumpet,' he shouted in a fearful voice and with a yell of maniac laughter plucked the pillow from her head and pressed it remorselessly upon her face, kneading it with all his force like dough. Her limbs quivered and writhed; she beat the air with aimless feeble hands.

'Down, strumpet, down . . .' he howled again and again whilst peal upon peal of hideous merriment rang through the house.

He flung the pillow from him. Her body fell limp and lifeless half out of the bed.

126

He stood there and laughed . . . and laughed . . . and laughed.

There were shouts and cries at the back of the stage. A stout old person—in a tall silk hat and evening dress whose expanse of stiff white shirt front and diamond studs glittered and shone; carpenters in their rough aprons, coatless and unkempt; somebody clutching a book and gesticulating wildly; a crowd of folk in tawdry quasi-romantic costumes, trunks and hose, poured on through the wings.

In front the audience were leaping to their feet. Women screamed and fainted. Men were hallooing and trying to scramble from their seats over the rails.

Sir Gilbert jumped up only to fall back, his senses reeling with the horror of the thing. Yet whilst he swooned that hellish laughter rang unceasingly in his ears above the uproar and the din, as the Moor stood there and laughed . . . and laughed . . . and laughed.

※

It was a very white and shaken guest who said good-bye to Mrs. Hunstanton some hours later, and it needed no unwonted courage on his part (I think) to have the Toy Theatre carefully packed and nailed up in a big wooden box. He was strangely silent on his way to the station, and it was not without considerable misgivings that Tom Hunstanton waved him farewell from the platform.

'Seemed regularly off colour,' subsequently remarked that gentleman to his wife. 'I can't understand it at all. He's been so fit all the time he's been down here with us.'

'Sicking for something, I'm afraid,' quoth the lady. 'He hardly touched any breakfast. Just before a journey too! You'd better write in a few days, Tom, and inquire how he is. I did ask him to stay if he wasn't well enough to travel, but he wouldn't hear of it. He put me off by sticking to it that it was nothing more than a headache. Anyway, I did ask him. Of course if he is in for an attack, and such I fear must be the case, it was very wise of him to get home as quickly as possible, for he had far better be there than here: were it anything serious it would have been most awkward for us two just when we are off to Town . . . Yes, I know, dear, but at any rate in a few days' time. I expect he felt that. I only hope he didn't catch anything in one of those nasty old shops at Caeravon.' And Mrs. Hunstanton was in one way much nearer to the truth than she guessed.

Upon his arrival rather latish that evening at Abbotsleigh—it is a fair cry from the Marches to Essex, and trains were not very adaptable—the box containing the Toy Theatre (without a nail being drawn) was by Sir Gilbert's direction carried to an attic where it was carefully sheeted whilst he locked the door upon it and put the key in his own breast pocket. By this time he very well recovered from his experience of the night before, and he felt sure that—whatever might be its cause—the phenomenon he had involuntarily witnessed was, so to speak, entirely local and focussed upon the Toy Theatre itself, no disturbance would be felt or noise heard in any adjoining room, for example, although even so persuaded he was not taking the remotest chances.

His next step was to endeavour to locate some explanation of so extraordinary not to say horrible a happening, and with the data at his disposal this did not prove very difficult an accomplishment.

It is not necessary to detail the steps by which owing to the medium of his friend the Librarian of the Kemble Collection Sir Gilbert was introduced to Mortimer Chalmers, a ripe old journalist of some threescore years and ten and a great authority on things theatrical.

'Romantzini? Oh, yes, I remember him quite well, even if I was not much more than a lad at the time,' said Chalmers meditatively as he stirred the lump of sugar in his warm brandy and water. 'Romantzini. It's rather a grim tale, and although it made a pretty stir in its day I fancy most of our stage historians, our Genests and Dorans, are content to let it lie forgotten. Besides he was only a Minor Theatre star. But if you're interested . . . his true name was Vitelleus Brown, and he hailed from the West Indies, I think. Yes, he was a coloured man—a genuine black. Anyhow, he made a great hit on the boards in New York, and came over to London as a novelty. The black Roscius, he was billed as. And a prize draw he turned out to be. London went plum crazy over him for a bit. There wasn't a lass in town who wasn't after him, and you could see his portrait stuck up in every shop. Lord, yes, it's all coming back to me now . . . Thank you, I will have another. The same, please . . . Here's your very good health, sir . . . What was I saying? Oh, yes, he was first rate in his own line. Very limited though. He did Oroonoko, and Langa, and Abdelazer, and Aaron in *Titus Andronicus*. Of course, Othello was his great part. Married? He married a young actress who had made her debut not very long before. They said she had money of her own, but I don't know anything about that. Anyhow, she was a lovely creature. I saw her Portia and Rosalinda and Cordelia, and half-a-dozen more. Fair and soft and clinging, she was. Let me see now . . . what was her name? I declare I've forgotten for the moment . . . but I shall remember presently . . . Emily . . . Emily . . .'

'Langrivier?'

'That's it, of course. Langrivier . . . Emily Langrivier. And they used to act together. Then I don't know how it was, I suppose the novelty wore off, and Romantzini or Vitelleus Brown began to find that his audiences were growing a bit thin. Somebody or something else came along—diving Lilliputians or Aztec Rope Dancers or the Myriozama—a new attraction anyhow. He'd been making money by the bushel, and spending it just as freely, for he liked to cut a dash, and for all his black skin he was as a peacock with the temper of a tiger. Why, when some fellow on *The Examiner* slated his Oroonoko, he found out who it was and half-murdered the poor chap. There was an awful row at the time, and he had to pay pretty heavily too, which didn't improve matters as things were already on the wane . . . Ah! . . . Well, I don't mind just one more . . . Thanks, yes, the same . . . Next he took it into his head that there was a cabal against him. Mind you, I don't believe there was, but they all do that. You daren't say so much as a hint of a criticism without there's a cry of clique—clique-clique! Have you never noticed it? Touchy kittle cattle actors. Then her manager wanted to put the Langrivier into Juliet and Belvidera and Jane Shore, and of course Romantzini couldn't play opposite to her in any of those. That set his back up to begin with—stupid, why yes, of course it was considering—if you're a Negro you can't play Romeo can you? At least not to a white Juliet . . . on the boards, I mean. Ha! Ha! Ha! So they engaged young Victor Everard, who they used to call the Thespian Adonis, and he was Romeo and Jaffier and the rest. Then there was more trouble. Romantzini couldn't stomach another man making love to his wife, not even on stage. He was mad with jealousy. Half-mad. And pretty soon rumours got about that Romeo and Juliet were lovers in private life as well. To make matters worse the pair always drew packed houses. And they deserved it. I've seen a good many Romeos and Juliets in my time, but never any to touch them. As to their being lovers . . . well, there's no doubt about that. You only had to watch them on the boards. It's an old story and it can't hurt anyone to say so now. This went on for some time, and a grand Easter season was announced at Bagnigge Wells—say was it Bagnigge Wells or the Adelaide? I forget, and anyhow it doesn't matter for the moment. If you want to know we can easily look it up. On Easter Monday they opened with *Othello*. Romantzini, Othello; the Langrivier, Desdemona; and Everard, Cassio. It was remarked that Romantzini seemed fearfully excited, but people thought that was because he was winning back his old laurels. He was at the top of his form and they cheered him to the echo, I've heard critics say they never saw such acting, and it wasn't altogether acting either. Well, in the bedroom scene he snatched up a pillow and smothered his wife—murdered her there and then—before the whole house. Ugh . . . They couldn't stop him . . . they didn't realise until it was just too late . . . you see it's in the play . . . There was something like a riot in the theatre after it . . . The people would have killed him if they could, and as it was they pretty well wrecked the house—smashed up everything. At any rate, that was an end of that theatre. Nobody had any success there. Mangers wouldn't touch it. Nobody would act in it. They pulled it down at last, not so many years after either . . . Only thing they could do . . . What happened to Romantzini? No, he wasn't hanged, although plenty of people said he ought to have been, for that same night Everard was found in his dressing-room with his throat cut from ear to ear. Of course it couldn't be proved, but it's fairly certain Romantzini slipped in during the last interval and did the trick. They took him away in a strait waistcoat, raving mad. So, as I said, they couldn't hang him. They could never get anything out of him. He just used to sit and laugh to himself all day long, I've heard. I remember one of the boys at the theatre telling me that he thought half the mischief had been brought about by Romantzini's dresser, a nasty sly sort of chap, always padding up and down and key-holing . . . but devoted to his master . . . thanks . . . yes . . . but a stirrup-cup it must be this time.'

※

I may add that—although he possessed several early and rare models—after Sir Gilbert's death no Toy Theatre, set for *Othello*, and answering the elaborate description in his Diary could be found, nor was there any record of this particular piece in his carefully written up catalogue. On being questioned (I fear at my instigation) by Jack Ritchie, Barnes the old butler remembered a large sheeted box which lay for years in the attic, and which 'the squire' would never allow to be touched or moved. But it has disappeared now, and one can only suppose that eventually Sir Gilbert took steps to ensure that nobody else should see—well, what he once saw.

The Grimoire

The snare is laid for him in the ground,
and a trap for him in the way.
Terrors shall make him afraid on every side.

'ANYTHING in my line today, Merritt?'

The bookseller, a spare, spectacled old man, looked up quickly from 'The Clique' which he was studying, blue pencil in hand, at his desk, and shot forward his scraggy neck not unlike the protruding head of some ancient tortoise, to peer hesitatingly through the half-gloom of his little shop. Even on this sunny afternoon it was not an over-light place, but shadowy and full of those dark nooks and mysterious corners stacked with bundles of dusty tomes such as the adventurer in old bookshops loves, where one hopes to find at last that uncut quarto play by D'Urfey, that elusive eighteenth-century pamphlet, or that novel of Eliza Haywood's for which one has been searching so patiently and so long.

'Good afternoon, sir. Why, yes, I have got something put aside for you. Only came in yesterday. I was posting you a card this evening about it.'

'Lucky I looked in, for I shouldn't have had time to call tomorrow as I'm off to Silchester for ten days or a fortnight. Let's see it.'

Mr. Merritt gingerly lowering himself from the high office-stool upon which he was perched, shambled towards a small glass-fronted Chippendale bookcase at the back of the shop. Taking a ring of labelled keys from his pocket he unlocked the door, and selected from among the array of morocco and calf-gilt bindings a podgy octavo vellum volume.

'There you are, sir.'

'Not another Bodin, I hope, or one of the later editions of the *Malleus* . . . ah, I see,' and the speaker did indeed see that he was handling something altogether uncommon and rare, since in spite of the fact that he had been a collector of books on alchemy, witchcraft and the occult sciences generally for a good many years he could not recollect ever before having come across the treatise whose title-page he was now scanning with such eager attention. Nor was it a work he would have been likely to forget. *Mysterium Arcanum, seu de daemonibus rite evocandis cum quibusdam aliis secretis abditissimis*, Romae, sine permissu superiorum. '*The Secret Mystery, or the Art of Evoking Evil Spirits with certain other Most Curious and Close Matters*, printed at Rome—that's fudge—no date, without the permission of the authorities. Well, whoever the writer was and I can't place him for the moment, he had a sense of humour at any rate. Early seventeenth-century printing I should guess. And the contents—they sound appetizing enough, but it may only be a hash-up of the Petit Albert and that wretched Pope Honorius.'

"As you say, sir. You know more about that sort of thing than I do. Anyhow, I think it's a scarce item, and I've had a good many of these books through my hands in the past five-and-twenty years. Yet it's the first time I've seen that one.'

'What date do you give it, Merritt?'

The bookseller took up the *Mysterium*, and moving to the door for a better light, held it within a few inches of his nose, blinking uncertainly. 'To tell the truth, sir, I haven't examined it closely. As soon as I saw it, I said to myself, "Now that's a bit for Dr. Hodsoll. Dr. Hodsoll will take that book." And so I snapped it up sharp.'

'And how much do you propose to stick Dr. Hodsoll for it, eh?'

Mr. Merritt, his head slightly inclined to one side, regarded the book for a minute in silence. 'Ah, if you're asking me for a figure, Doctor, I am telling you that I should catalogue this item at six guineas, not a penny less. But I am going to let you have it for five.'

Dr. Hodsoll and Mr. Merritt were old friends, but a histrionic palaver seemed called for by the occasion.

'Come,' said Hodsoll, turning over the leaves carelessly, here we have a book with no date and a sham imprint, which is very probably as I've just said not much more than an adaptation of Solomon's Clavicule'—and as he spoke he lied and he knew that he lied, but such are the ways of collectors—'and you are going to ask me five pounds for it. Pooh!'

'Five guineas, sir, guineas.'

'That's worse. Hang it all, Merritt, it's buying a pig in a poke.'

'Well, sir, if you don't think it's worth that to you
. . . but I made sure you'd like it for your collection, that
is supposing you already haven't a copy. I shan't keep it
long, anyhow. I expect Mr. Spicer will be interested,'
and the wily old man made as if to return the little
volume to its shelf.

At the mention of his rival's name, Dr. Hodsoll bris-
tled like a porcupine, and quickly put out a restraining
hand. 'Here, not so quick, Merritt,' he cried, 'let's have
another peep at it first.'

A very cursory glance sufficed. Five notes and two
half-crowns exchanged hands, and whilst a neat parcel was being made, Dr. Hodsoll queried: 'Look here,
Merritt, you said it only came in yesterday, didn't you?
Have you any objection to my asking where it came
from?'

'Not the slightest, sir, only I'm afraid I can't tell you
much. A young fellow, quite a stranger to me, brought
it in. just before closing time, and asked me what I'd
give for it there and then. So I bought it over the counter, as you may say.'

'Ah! Well, I only wondered. No question it's an out-
of-the-way book.'

'Shall we send it round, sir? You shall have it within
the next half-hour.'

'No, I can carry it. I'm going straight home. I'll take
it with me.'

As a matter of fact, Dr. Hodsoll did not go straight
home, for less than a couple of hundred yards from
the book-shop he was buttonholed by a bore of the
first water, from whom he could not escape without

a promise of lunch at an early date. The delay caused him to fall straight into the arms of Miss Matty Davies, whom he must needs squire to her garden gate—it was not so very far out of his way, as she remarked, and she was sure he would be interested to know about the doings and mis-doings of her new maid. 'Ah, once servants were servants,' she said, with a shake of her crisp, grey curls, 'and now——!'

The result was that by the time he put his latch-key in his own front door the clock of St. Matthew's at the corner of the road had struck half-past six some minutes before, and simultaneously with his entrance there appeared in the hall the excellent Burkitt, who ministered so admirably to his creature comforts and who was (be it whispered) a little bit of a tyrant in his way, to remind his master that he was dining at a house three miles distant and it behoved him not to loiter in the study over his letters and paper if he intended to be anything like punctual. In consequence the new purchase had to be put on the table, and Dr. Hodsoll dared not trust himself to open it before he went up to dress. He left it, however, with a promise to do something more than dip into it on his return before he went to sleep, a promise that was never fulfilled since the dinner was longer and more formal, the company larger, and he got back considerably later than he had expected, feeling not a little tired and very ready for bed.

The next morning Dr. Hodsoll proved quite unable to do such ample justice as his wont, in fact to do justice at all, to the tempting breakfast Mrs. Burkitt sent up from her well-ordered kitchen. He turned aside from kidneys and bacon, York ham and new-laid eggs alike, only able to manage a little dry toast with his tea. He had passed a restless and disturbed night, which left him curiously inert and depressed. He was a sound sleeper—he used to boast that he fell asleep as soon as his head touched the pillow and that he never knew anything more until eight o'clock next morning—yet not only had he tossed and turned and counted numberless sheep quite unavailingly, but when he did doze off he dreamed, and his dreams were of a singularly unpleasant nature. True they partook of that seemingly incoherent nature which appears a general characteristic of dreams, and he had, as is not infrequent, a very vague and confused memory of them upon waking, but in each there was the recurrent figure of a man, the same man, who in some way persisted and returned quite clearly every time he had closed his eyes. The man was an ordinary figure enough—he had never been able to catch sight of his face—but in some way he realized that this visitant was evil and wished him ill. The curious part was that the man seemed to be loitering up and down the corridor outside his bedroom and on the landing beyond. He had even stood outside the door with his ear bent to the keyhole listening to what was going on within. In fact, once this seemed so vivid that waking with a start Dr. Hodsoll had switched on the light, and jumping out of bed unbolted the door and flung it wide open. Of course there was nobody there, and he got back again conscious that he was more than a trifle ashamed of himself.

As he drank his last cup of tea—he was feeling particularly thirsty—and gazed out on to his gay flower-beds and smooth green lawn he passed in review his dietary of the day and particularly of the evening before, but he was unable to accuse himself of any especial indiscretion. A plain and careful liver, last night he had pointedly eschewed that rich-looking trifle with the avalanche of cream spangled with hundreds and thousands and chosen the more wholesome apples and rice. He had taken sole rather than the lobster cutlets, and avoided the mushroom savoury. No, he had nothing then with which to reproach himself. Perhaps he was ailing for something. If so Canon Spenlow wouldn't want an invalid in his house. Dr. Hodsoll crossed to a mirror and gravely examined his tongue. That looked all right at all events. Should he ring up little Dillon, and be overhauled before he went? (I should explain that Julian Hodsoll was a Doctor of Literature and not a physician). Just because he had happened to have had a bad night! It would never do to get so old-womanish. What could it be but indigestion? He had no headache, and no temperature. It was only this stupid laziness. Perhaps he had been overdoing it a bit lately. Well, at Silchester he would take a regular holiday, and slack. It was a soothing, restful place. The Canon was a model host, too, he let one do just as one liked so long as one attended a couple of services on Sunday. Of course that always became rather a bore, but then the music at the Cathedral was invariably first-rate. Why, to please the old fellow he wouldn't mind turning up two or three times on week-days during his visit. Ten o'clock or ten-thirty, he forgot which. It was worth it. Undoubtedly Silchester would do him all the good in the world.

Canon Spenlow, the only son of a wealthy Birmingham manufacturer (long since deceased), although a bachelor, kept up a large and rather old-fashioned household. Of extremely conservative views, he belonged to what was once known as the 'high and dry school' of thought, and was altogether an entirely correct and proper old gentleman, who profoundly distrusted both innovations or enthusiasms of any kind. The narrowness of his intellectual outlook was to a large extent modified, it is true, by his love of books and a keen interest in ecclesiastical archaeology, and it was at a meeting of a learned Society some years before that he had first met Dr. Hodsoll, to find that although he strongly disapproved of the laxity, not to say the scepticism, of his new friend's opinions, they had many tastes and pursuits in common. An invitation to Silchester resulted, since when several visits had been exchanged. The acquaintanceship was in one sense per-force rather one-sided, for Dr. Hodsoll could not very well enter into and indeed had small sympathy with the Canon's most intimate convictions, but he was both tactful and shrewd, and with the interests they had in common their talk of books, their cult of antiquity, they did very well.

It was rather late on an afternoon towards the end of April that Dr. Hodsoll's taxi turned into Silchester Close, and as he looked out of his window he saw with great satisfaction and content the large, square, red-brick house, built by some old churchman in the reign of the second James, and mellowed to an august beauty during the passage of years. The westering sun was brightly reflected in the many tall and narrow windows, whose little panes twinkled like very diamonds. The calm nobility and stateliness of the frontage pleased and soothed him, as did the gates of elaborate iron scroll work, the broad smooth path of yellow gravel beyond, sweeping round the velvety grass with its close and sombre shrubberies until it ended in a wide oval at the foot of the imposing flight of steps that led up to the great double door.

His friend welcomed him with evident pleasure, and after an elaborately planned and served dinner—for Canon Spenlow would bate no jot of his punctiliousness because they were only two at table, and both butler and footman were required to be in attendance—they settled down to a long and chatty evening in the library, a room of magnificent proportions lined from floor to ceiling with books. Here the latest treasures had to be exhibited and commented upon and admired. The bright fire blazing merrily away was grateful on the spring night; the arm-chairs were comfortable, neither too luxurious, nor too small; the port was of the finest vintage; the Canon had acquired some genuine rarities, including several incunabula; the topics of conversation were many and varied. Midnight struck as the host was taking down yet another recent treasure trove from his shelves. 'Oh! Dear me!' he exclaimed, 'twelve o'clock already. Who would have thought it? But I mustn't be inconsiderate, my dear Hodsoll, and keep you from your bed. Because I'm a late sitter it doesn't follow that you are. One last glass of port? No? A brandy and soda, then? Nothing more? Ah, well, perhaps you are wise. And I think we'll be turning in. If I may say so, you are not looking quite so robust as I've seen you, and perhaps I've been to blame in detaining you so late as it is.'

'Not at all, Canon, not at all. Truth to tell I had rather a restless night last night, and I shouldn't be speaking honestly if I were to say that I didn't feel a trifle tired after my journey.'

'Travel by train is always fatiguing, I think. And personally I've never found myself able to prefer a car. But if you are not thoroughly rested tomorrow morning, take your breakfast in bed, I beg. You only have to ring or tell the servant who calls you. Perhaps you would rather not be called until a somewhat later hour?'

'No, no. I couldn't think of disturbing your arrangements. Breakfast in bed I particularly dislike. If I'm not well enough to get up, I'm not well enough to eat any breakfast. It is like your kindness to suggest it, but believe me there's not the slightest occasion for anything of the sort.'

'You'll join me at breakfast at nine-thirty then? Good. You shall be called at eight-thirty. Myself, I am celebrating the Eucharist at eight o'clock, and I hardly suppose I shall have returned from the Cathedral much before nine. Good-night, and good sound sleep.'

'Good-night, Canon.'

When Canon Spenlow came back from the Cathedral after his celebration in the Lady Chapel he found Dr. Hodsoll walking in the garden 'to clear his pipes' as Sir Roger has it, breathing the air in great lung-fulls, and watching the rooks circling about the old grey towers that pierced the somewhat watery blue, across which raced a cavalcade of fleecy white clouds. After the usual matutinal greetings and inquiries the cleric congratulated his guest with 'I declare the change has done you good already.'

'I'm inclined to think it has,' was the sanguine reply, 'certainly your cloister air is an admirable sedative. I never felt better in my life.'

The morning post brought the Canon a budget of correspondence and several book-catalogues, and as Dr. Hodsoll was indulging his bad habit of dipping into *The Times* at table, the two men exchanged only a few remarks during breakfast until towards the end of the meal when the Canon, who had been glancing through a letter with an Italian stamp and post-mark, looked up and said, 'I hope you don't mind, Hodsoll, beyond a dinner with the Dean, who wouldn't take a refusal, I've not made any social engagements during your visit.'

'Nothing could suit me better, Canon. I am looking forward for one thing to going through some of those books again which you showed me last night. I should like to make a note or two, for example, on that early edition of Condrochius, and I'm not so well acquainted with Pordage and Jane Lead as I hope to be after a day or two in your library, for I see you have the *Mystic Divinite* and *A Fountain of Gardens* on your shelves.'

'Quaint old mystics both,' the Canon smiled. 'But it all fits in very well, because most mornings when I get back from Mattins, I am generally busy in the library until lunch, and I know that's the time you prefer for your stroll round Silchester. I take my constitutional in the afternoon, and you can have the library entirely to yourself and browse among your visionaries as long as you please. However, I was going to say that one reason why I have declined invitations during the next few days is owing to another guest of mine who will join us on Monday. I have just had a letter,' holding up the thin foreign envelope, 'from him to that effect.'

'Indeed? Is it anyone whom I know?'

'Not as yet. But it is someone whom, if I mistake not, you will be very interested to meet. A Dominican friar. You are surprised,' for Dr. Hodsoll had indeed looked up wonderingly, 'but when I was in Rome last year Father Raphael Grant showed me several kindnesses, and opened doors for me which would otherwise most certainly have remained shut. He is a very able historian, and naturally he is keenly interested in the annals of his own particular order. When I told him of the cartularies and the manuscript missal which at the Dissolution passed from the Blackfriars here to the Cathedral Library—you will remember, no doubt, that they were only discovered, or to speak more precisely, recognized a few years ago, I had an article upon them, which you may have read, in the *Ecclesiastical Review*—he expressed himself as extremely desirous of examining them in detail, and then of course there are the other codices and registers. I can be of some assistance to him there, I am glad to say, and although he is only able to spare a very few days it will be far more convenient for him to be staying here than it would be if he had to go among strangers.'

'I am sure I shall very much look forward to meeting him,' rejoined Hodsoll. 'When do you expect your guest?'

'On Monday, so his letter says,' answered the Canon. 'You will find him a very intellectual, and I think I may quite safely add a very charming companion.'

The morning passed pleasantly enough, but without incident. Dr. Hodsoll strolled rather aimlessly through the narrow streets and cobbled winds (as they are locally called) of the city; he renewed his acquaintance with the old Buttermarket and Sorrowing Cross; drew blank at a couple of book-shops; peeped into St. Bennet, Eastgate and St. Mildred's, shuddering at the garish magenta and gamboge window with which some pious mayor of the late Victorian seventies had outraged the latter; exchanged a word or two with the curator of the Museum; and made his way through the shadowy aisles of the Cathedral back to lunch.

Then followed two hours of unalloyed bliss in the library, where about four o'clock the Canon joined him for a cup of tea. The conversation, as we may suppose, was of books, and books, and books again.

'Yes, I acknowledge I have had one or two quite lucky finds lately,' said Canon Spenlow, 'but on the other, hand I had to give its full price for that Tacitus, and a good deal more than its full price for the *Don Quixote*. But what of yourself, Hodsoll, haven't you come across anything special recently? I always say I never knew a man who had the knack of picking up what he wanted in the same way as you manage to hunt your quarry down. And while the rest of us are giving preposterous figures and rummaging and ferreting you just go round the corner, and hey presto! There it is.'

Dr. Hodsoll laughed as he knocked out his pipe, and replied: 'I'm afraid you exaggerate, Canon. Whatever may have been the case years ago, it's all different today. Not a bargain to be had! Even Merritt's prices are soaring. Only a couple of days ago he asked me five guineas for a book—and got it. By the way, I should like to show it to you, and perhaps you could help me to trace it. It's something of an oddity. I've brought it with me, and it won't take a minute to fetch it.'

No sooner said than done, and Hodsoll handed the Canon the little parcel intact just as he had received it over Merritt's counter. 'There you are,' he said, I haven't even had time to look through it carefully. Open it, and see if you can tell me anything about the book.'

The Canon unknotted the string with some precision and tidily folded the paper before he turned to the title-page of the podgy vellum octavo. He stared, took off his glasses and carefully wiped them before proceeding to a second inspection. 'Extraordinary!' he exclaimed. 'That's highly interesting. Can it be some sort of a joke? A polemic? A burlesque?'

'Oh, no. I hardly think so. At any rate, it doesn't extend farther than the imprint. The writer was in deadly earnest, I feel sure.'

'Ah! so it seems.' As Canon Spenlow turned the pages, scanning a paragraph here and there a heavy frown gathered upon his brow. 'God bless my soul! Why, wherever did you get this thing?'

'From Merritt, as I told you. He bought it from a casual seller, and I bought it from him the very next day. Have you ever seen a copy before?'

'No, and God forbid I should ever see a copy again.' The old man shut the book sharply, and slapped it down on a table with the utmost distaste. 'Have you examined it, have you read it, Hodsoll?'

'No, not yet. I am looking forward——'

'Then take my advice and forgive me for speaking frankly. Put it behind the fire. Nay, I am certain you will do so when you read it.'

Dr. Hodsoll stood petrified. 'Put it behind the fire! Why, it may be unique. At any rate, I'm sure it's of the last rarity.'

'Thank God for that. I am quite serious. Never have I seen in print such filth, such appalling blasphemy.'

'Oh, I know some of these demonologists are a trifle strong, but——'

'It's not a question of being a trifle strong. Read, man, read for yourself.' The Canon was deeply moved.

In some surprise Hodsoll took up the offending volume to discover the cause of so unexpected an outburst. Nor had he long to search. The very page to which he turned seemed to be some kind of liturgical ceremony, there were prayers addressed to the powers of darkness in terms of hideous profanity and rubrics of the most crapulous obscenity. What a blunder to have shown that to Canon Spenlow! He must be diplomatic and smooth the old fellow down.

'Whew!' he ejaculated, 'that's pretty bad. I assure you, Canon, I had no idea there was anything like this.

148

I'm sorry. Yet as a matter of curiosity, or rather from a bibliographical point of view, I think one ought to set on record a full description of this fellow, lewd and degraded as he is.'

'Personally I should burn it here and now,' retorted the Canon. 'But, of course, it's not my property. It's an evil book.'

'I shall certainly follow your advice. Yet I think it would be a mistake not to have a memorandum of it, and perhaps a photograph of the title-page which, you must admit, is singular.'

Canon Spenlow made an impatient noise, and, pointing a long lean finger, quoted vigorously: 'Many of them also which used curious arts brought their books together, and burned them before all men: and they counted the price of them, and found it fifty thousand pieces of silver.'

These were regions into which Dr. Hodsoll was quite unable to follow his friend, and he therefore contented himself with a murmured 'Quite,' which he felt none the less to be inappropriate and inconclusive.

At that moment there came a not unwelcome interruption in the shape of the butler with a note for his master, a missive which required an immediate answer, and Hodsoll, hastily gathering up his book lest it should be seized for a holocaust, was glad to escape to the fastness of his bedroom where, bolting the door behind him, he sank into an arm-chair, feeling breathless and flurried.

'Phew!' he exclaimed, mopping his brow with his handkerchief, 'whoever could have supposed that the old chap would flare up like that! It's just it, you never know with these religious folk where you are going to have 'em. And now let's see what all the bother's about.'

He was soon obliged to confess that the contents of the *Mysterium Arcanum* were sufficiently startling. There were a number of charms, a few to constrain love, others to compel hate, and some with a yet more definitely atrocious aim, '*capitis damnatio*', the 'death warrants', they were termed. There were receipts for poison, and philters of the foulest ingredients. Next followed evocations of demons, cantrips and spells, and three sections entitled respectively 'the way of Cain', 'the error of Balaam', and 'the gainsaying of Core'. There were litanies addressed to the fallen archangel as the patron of every licence and abomination. There were prayers to the powers of the pit *ante et post missam*, and a rubric which set Hodsoll wondering, *missam autem quaere apud Missale Nigrum* (the Mass itself will be found in the Black Missal).

Could it be that the mysterious book of the witches had fallen into his hands, that volume which was mentioned in more than one trial of the seventeenth century, but which apparently had never been seen by any who was not a member of that horrid society? The *Mysterium Arcanum* showed at any rate the signs of constant use. In the margins, here and there, an old hand had jotted various notes and drawn strange cabalistic signs. And to his delight he saw that a blank page at the end was covered with fine close writing headed *Evocatio efficacissima*, a most Powerful and Efficacious

150

Evocation. 'Crabbed, contracted Latin! Well, I suppose I shall have to transcribe this at length, and the sooner I do it the better.' Uncapping his fountain pen, and taking a quire of quarto paper from his case, Dr. Hodsoll set to work, and before long had written out in full the impious and unhallowed charm. In order to check it carefully and make sure he had omitted no word nor syllable, he then read it through sentence by sentence softly to himself.

There came a light tap at the door, and he actually started. 'The servant with hot water, How time flies! I must change at once.' Hastily shuffling the book and his manuscript under a sheet of blotting-paper, he called over his shoulder, 'Come in.'

'You wanted me, sir,' said a low voice.

Dr. Hodsoll turned and saw that there had entered the room and was standing waiting his orders a tall young man with the impassive features and formal bearing of the well-trained servant. He was dressed, not in livery, but in a smartly-cut black suit, and seemed the very pattern of a gentleman's valet. At the same time there was something foreign in his appearance, which was perhaps due to his large dark eyes, full of infinite sadness and a yearning regret, and the extreme pallor of his countenance.

'Another valet of the Canon's,' thought Hodsoll. 'Really he has more servants just to look after himself than would be needed to wait on a family. But I suppose he entertains a good deal in this large house.' Then aloud, 'No, thanks, I didn't ring. I need nothing until my hot water comes.'

'I beg your pardon, sir, I thought you wanted me,' and the servant withdrew.

Dr. Hodsoll, reflecting that the Canon would not care for the *Mysterium* to be left about, although certainly none of the household could read Latin, and the book was quite safe unless indeed from a conscientious scruple his host purloined and destroyed it, locked it away in a suit-case. He was glad he had done so, for as he went downstairs he noticed the valet loitering in the passage not far from his door, and in these days of universal education who knows, he asked himself, whether this chap hasn't taken a course in classics and reads Horace or Livy in the servants' hall.

The Canon, he was relieved to find, made no allusion either covert or direct to the *Mysterium*, and the evening passed tranquilly, closing however at a rather earlier hour in view of the morrow being a Sunday. Upon entering his bedroom and switching on the light Hodsoll was surprised and a little annoyed to find the valet awaiting him.

'What do you want?' he asked rather abruptly.

'I was waiting for you, sir,' was the reply in perfectly courteous and even deferential tones. 'What can I do for you?'

'Nothing at all,' answered Hodsoll. 'I will ring if I require anything more.' The man bowed, and left the room quietly, yet Hodsoll had the curious impression that he caught an extremely ugly look just as he was going out 'What on earth's the matter with the fellow?' he asked himself. 'Is he afraid he won't get a tip when I leave. And he certainly won't if he bothers me like this. Ugh! I'm beginning to hate the sight of him,' and he unbuttoned his waistcoat impatiently. 'Why, he must have been up here in the dark, because the light certainly wasn't burning until I turned it on. Well, that's odd.'

The next morning Canon Spenlow noticed that his guest was looking far from well, but an inquiry only elicited the information that he had passed a restless night, and as he saw that further questioning began to irritate he refrained from pressing the matter. He was somewhat agreeably surprised, however, to find that Dr. Hodsoll would not listen to his suggestion of staying away from the Morning Service at the Cathedral. In fact, he showed himself eager to attend, and at the luncheon table he spoke with a show of sympathy and understanding which he had never expressed before of the comfort and consolation those who hold the Christian faith derive from common worship and the beauty of an ordered liturgy.

That afternoon, the Canon being otherwise engaged, Dr. Hodsoll, when Evensong was over, decided to take a stroll through the meadows which lined the river's bank. Although unenclosed, these had for the extent of nearly half a mile been turned into a public garden from which one passed almost insensibly into the open country and lanes which lay beyond. There were seats, and thick hedges which formed a kind of natural wall, and although just about tea-time on a Sunday afternoon the meadows were almost empty, later in the evening when dusk began to fall and the stars crept out they would be dotted with trysting couples, since the Meads had for generations been the recognized rendezvous of every Silchester lass who was 'walking out' with her young man.

Feeling tired, after a few turns Dr. Hodsoll sat down upon a bench which had been placed in a natural arbour, facing the view which for all its familiarity never lost its charm—the old huddled roofs of the city, the Cathedral towers, the sedgy banks with the stream gently flowing between. He had not been seated many minutes when he felt a sense of extreme uneasiness and disquiet; he shuddered violently as though some horrible thing was near and, as he afterwards declared, he was filled with the apprehension that a wild beast lurked in ambush ready to leap out and tear him piecemeal. In vain he tried to concentrate his thoughts on other things, books, a monograph he was contemplating, a forthcoming visit to Buxton, to call common sense to his aid. At last unable to endure the tension longer he jumped to his feet almost to ward off a blow, and as he half-turned he saw staring at him through the bushes with an expression so evil and malevolent that even now the very memory has cost him more than one sleepless night, a dead-white face in which the great dark eyes blazed like hot coals of fire. The face was instantly withdrawn. In fact, it vanished so swiftly that if he had not recognized it he might have believed it was mere imagination, a trick and play of light and shadow among the leaves. He returned to the house considerably shaken, and then, I think, that he must first have suspected who the servant was.

The next incident which seems worthy of record took place about ten o'clock that same evening when without so much as a preliminary knock or a word of warning the door of the housekeeper's room burst open, and Lucy Parkins, the Canon's upper housemaid, rushed in and almost collapsed at Mrs. Bailey's feet. That extremely correct and punctilious lady, who was reading her Chapter before the fire and sipping a glass of mulled claret preparatory to retiring to bed, arose stately from her chair, every fold of her black satin dress rustling in stern displeasure. 'What can be the meaning of this, Parkins?' she began in freezing tones. 'Have you taken leave of your senses?' and then, for she saw that the girl was white with terror and sobbing hysterically, she added more quickly, 'What is it, you stupid girl, what has happened?'

'Oh, Mrs. Bailey, ma'am,' exclaimed Parkins, 'I am so frightened. I don't know what to do. Indeed I don't.'

'Frightened? Shut that door at once, and tell me all about it.' Then seeing the girl was shaking and shivering, Mrs. Bailey closed the door, and pushed her into a chair. From her own private cupboard she administered a small glass of brandy, and when she saw the colour coming back into her cheeks, she sharply commanded: 'Stop that yammering now and tell me what's frightened you.'

The upshot of Parkins' story was that she had come in at ten o'clock as usual after her Sunday evening out, and in the passage leading to the kitchen a strange man had brushed by her and looked at her horribly, he was just horrible, as she expressed it, and she had felt so terrified that she made for the shelter of Mrs. Bailey's room as a haven of safety. No amount of questioning and cross-examination on the housekeeper's part could shake her story.

'It's all those silly films. Wicked, I call it, allowing those places to be open on a Sunday night and filling the girls' and the young men's heads with trash, as though there wasn't enough badness in the world already,' indignantly declared the ruffled matron, somewhat more perturbed and puzzled than she cared to admit, for Lucy Parkins had always been a most staid and sensible worker. It transpired too that so far from having spent the evening at the cinema, she had been to supper at the house of her uncle, a small shopkeeper of eminent respectability. Eventually Mr. Watson, the butler, was summoned from his pantry to hear the tale, and although evidently not believing in Parkins' strange man, he undertook to go round the lower regions of the house to make sure all windows were closed and that no burglar was lurking in a cupboard or behind a door to issue forth in the night and cut all their throats. A clean bill of safety being returned, Parkins was dismissed to her bedroom, which was fortunately shared by the second maid, 'for sleep in the room alone tonight, I would not, no, not if anyone was to pay me thousands,' she pathetically declared.

'Now, stop that nonsense, and get to bed, you want a good night's rest, Lucy,' was Mr. Watson's unsympathetic reply.

'All the same it's funny, I must say, Mr. Watson,' remarked Mrs. Bailey, gazing after the departing Parkins, 'I've never known her took like this before, and she's a good worker too.'

'Bilious, Mrs. Bailey, bilious. That's what it is, depend upon it.'

'Well, I hope to goodness we're not going to have her in bed tomorrow, with this new gentleman coming, and all. I half wish I'd made her take a dose of salts or a pill.'

Had Dr. Hodsoll confided his suspicions to Canon Spenlow I am of opinion that his story would have been received with a far greater understanding and sympathy than he imagined, but the fact remains that fearing to look a fool, he chose rather to suffer, and there can be no doubt that he suffered very acutely on that Sunday night. Although actually the servant did not re-appear—he believed he caught a glimpse of him once, a shadowy figure, at the end of a corridor—he felt that he was being closely watched and that if he was off his guard for a moment, there would come a pounce. That the Canon guessed something was amiss is evident from the reluctance with which Hodsoll said good-night, and the earnestness with which he asked for his friend's prayers.

The next morning in the course of his walk round Silchester, Dr. Hodsoll turned into the Adam and Eve, the oldest hostelry in the city and one much frequented and admired by tourists. He drank no less than four glasses of their famous brown sherry, but the waiter remarked that although at first he seemed inclined to loiter he left very abruptly upon the entrance of another customer, and what was more curious the newcomer seemed to have followed him out immediately. Perhaps he had come there to seek him, at any rate he did not wait to be served.

The rest of the morning Dr. Hodsoll spent in the Cathedral. Father Raphael Grant to whom he was introduced at the luncheon-table did not at all fulfil his idea of a Dominican. True he was dressed in a white habit with leathern girdle and black scapular, and a rosary hung at his side. But he had neither the commanding stature nor proud port of an Inquisitor. His face was not emaciated and thin, burning with the fanatic fires of a Savonarola. It was in fact rather round and fresh-coloured, whilst his eyes twinkled humorously behind his gold-rimmed glasses. He was merely a courtly, extremely well-informed English gentleman who for some reason of his own chose to wear a picturesque and mediaeval attire.

The talk which at first naturally turned upon the treasures of Silchester Cathedral and the manuscripts Father Raphael particularly wished to collate, soon began to range over the whole field of literature and it was evident that the friar had worked in most of the big European libraries.

'By the way, Hodsoll,' remarked Canon Spenlow, towards the end of the meal, 'I took the liberty of mentioning to Father Raphael that very extraordinary little book you picked up recently and which you showed me the other day. He is very anxious to see it, and I'm sure you will have no objection to letting us examine it.'

'Oh, no, naturally, not at all,' Hodsoll was conscious that he had blushed guiltily and was almost betrayed into a stammer, 'I shall be most pleased to show it to you. Certainly, yes. Only . . . or . . . I ought perhaps to warn Father Raphael . . . to say . . . that is, I . . .'

'You are afraid, Dr. Hodsoll, that it will be something of a shock?' asked Father Raphael. 'Please make yourself perfectly easy on that account. After all,' with a smile, 'you didn't write it, and you can't be held responsible for the contents, however unpleasant they may be.'

'Father Raphael may be able to tell you something of its origin,' interpolated the Canon, 'he has a knowledge of these things, and I think you would be very well advised to let him see it. Nay, I make the request as a personal favour to myself.'

'Oh, of course, Canon, of course. If you put it that way. And I am sure that Father Raphael quite understands . . .'

The Dominican bowed courteously without speaking.

'Then, if you will excuse me, I'll fetch it for you now.'

'Bring it into the library, Hodsoll, where we are going to have coffee,' said the Canon.

Dr. Hodsoll was coming downstairs, a little quickly perhaps, the *Mysterium Arcanum* in one hand, when from an angle of a landing, a rather dark spot even on the sunniest day, there seemed to leap out at him a black shapeless shadow, and it was only by fast clutching the balusters that he avoided an abrupt and dangerous fall. When he had steadied himself, and turned to look, he saw nothing.

The Dominican attentively scanned the pages of the vellum octavo Hodsoll had handed him. His expression did not alter in any degree of astonishment or distaste. It was merely the calm, careful scrutiny of a scholar examining a rare and curious work. Once he nodded to himself as he came across some phrase or passage which seemed not unfamiliar.

'Yes, Dr. Hodsoll,' he said at length, as he closed the *Mysterium*, and placed it on the table, 'you certainly have there a most scarce and uncommon book. It will perhaps seem to you an impertinence on my part if I proffer any comment on the nature and purpose of this treatise, and yet I must risk your displeasure. I cannot see anyone standing in such deadly peril without a word of warning on my part, a word I trust you will not take amiss. Believe me when I say in all seriousness that I had rather put a lighted match to a train of gunpowder than pronounce certain of these incantations. The very possession of the book is apt to bring you into most undesirable company.'

My impression is that Dr. Hodsoll was a good deal upset as well as not a little perplexed by the friar's words. On the one hand he shuddered to think that already he might, however unwittingly, have attracted attentions on the part of those whom he would certainly be most desirous to avoid, yet of whose existence philosophically he was far from resting assured. The incidents he had observed were (he argued) in themselves quite capable of a natural explanation and possibly merely subjective. A man who had always prided himself upon his mental poise and balance, who boasted in religious matters a 'healthy agnosticism', to use his own pet phrase, he was loath to confess his fears to another. Ridicule or polite incredulity he would beyond anything have resented. There was also the powerful motive of the book, which, as a bibliophile, he could hardly bring himself to destroy. It might be cased in morrocco, yes; and kept in a locked bookcase, certainly; but to burn these pages which were not impossibly unique, was unthinkable.

Begging to be excused on account of certain duties, Father Raphael Grant retired early to his room that evening, fortunately not to sleep.

Dr. Hodsoll and the Canon parted company somewhere past eleven o'clock, and it was with a sensation of relief that the former as he switched on his electric light saw there was no intruder in his bedchamber. A small but cheerful fire was burning in his grate, and after undressing somewhat slowly he slipped a dressing-gown over his sleeping-suit, and sat down to review the situation. It was only natural that two clerics such as Canon Spenlow and the friar, each in his own line of extremely orthodox views, should regard such a book as the *Mysterium* with abhorrence, and speak out pretty freely concerning it. No doubt he himself had been a little off-colour lately and fanciful, and he had allowed himself first to be vexed by and then to weave a regular romance around the officiousness of a new and over-zealous valet, who doubtless had been specially ordered to look after guests in the house. Add to that the mere accident of an ugly tramp having peered round a bush at him when he was tired and half-asleep, and—why he was yawning already. It was striking twelve.

As he turned towards the bed he saw standing but a few paces behind him the servant, and at that moment his heart chilled with deadly paralyzing terror, for in a flash he knew who he was and whence he came. Only a few seconds can have passed before the stranger spoke in low tones of horrid menace, but those seconds seemed to Hodsoll a fearful eternity, and it is fairly clear that he came as near to madness as a man may and not wholly lose his reason.

'You wanted me, sir.'

'No . . . no . . . no . . . go away !'

'You called me, fool. And do you think I am to be dismissed so lightly?'

His eyes blazing furiously with exulting hate, and crooking his lithe white hands which to his horror Hodsoll saw were armed with great sharp horny nails that curved like the cruel talons of a vulture or some foul beast of prey, the demon suddenly and silently leaped upon the unfortunate wretch, who, frantic with physical fear and an even intenser mental loathing, reeled backwards uttering a hoarse stifled cry.

In that moment the door was flung wide open and the Dominican friar advanced stern and unflinching into the room. Around his neck hung a purple stole, as with upraised hand he marked swift sacred signs in the air and spoke certain Latin words of might in a tone of imperious command. Hodsoll, who extremely dislikes being questioned about the incident, on one occasion acknowledged that he really remembers nothing of what transpired. He can only recall that he heard the Most Holy Name, and that with a moan of brute agony his assailant seemed to slip away—as he expressed it—into nothingness.

As may be supposed the struggle aroused the house, and the Canon followed by Watson and a footman in a state of *déshabillé* very shortly appeared on the scene. Father Raphael, however, was able completely to re-assure them by briefly stating that Dr. Hodsoll had been taken ill, but that he was better, and since he himself intended to pass the night in his room no further assistance would be necessary or required.

If I am not much mistaken, on the following day the Canon was privately enlightened as to the correct state of affairs by the Dominican, to whom Hodsoll confided the whole story. At any rate, the *Mysterium Arcanum* was burnt to ashes that morning, a cremation at which the Canon expressed highest satisfaction.

It does not require a very active imagination to appreciate why Julian Hodsoll, the cultured and intellectual agnostic, fasts much and prays, and a Tertiary of the Order wears around his neck against his skin the brown scapulary of Carmel.

Romeo and Juliet

Souvent j'écoute encor quand le chant a cessé.
—Saint-Lambert

'WHAT a beautiful creature!'
'Yes, she was a very beautiful creature,' answered Raymond as he glanced up for a moment from the canvas at which he was working.

'Were you in love with her?'

'I think we were all in love with her.'

'Did you paint her?'

'Twice. But the portraits are not here—they are neither of them in London—in fact, one of them is not in England. But you'll find a number of pencil-sketches of her in that portfolio . . . yes, the green one . . . Indeed I shouldn't be surprised if there's nothing but her amongst the whole lot . . . Of course, some of them are mere scratches, and none of them—not even the portraits I did, and they are far and away my best work—can give you the slightest idea of her marvellous and unearthly look . . . there was something spiritual about her . . . something not of this world . . . something which a great master alone could have caught with his brush. Perhaps only Angelico da Fiesole could have painted her.'

'Here she is—at least, I think . . . yes, it's the same face . . . here she is, dressed as a Swiss peasant—a charming costume—and, why here she is in a page's hose and jerkin . . . How exquisitely graceful! Who was she? Was she an actress?'

'Can't you guess?'

'Somehow the face seems familiar.'

'I think you must have seen portraits of her—have read about her at some time.'

'I have a vague idea . . . but I can't . . . oh, who is she?'

'See if the name is pencilled anywhere.'

'Here we are! Cecilia Bressan.'

'Yes . . . it's Cecilia Bressan.'

'Did you know her well, Raymond?'

'Very well indeed. In fact, I suppose at one time I was her most intimate friend.'

'Is it very dreadful? I'm afraid she's not much more than a name to me.'

'No? Ah, well, I expect most people have forgotten her by this time. After all, fifteen years is a long time ago. Now and again a musical critic compares some new prima donna with La Bressan—whom he never heard, and of whom he knows less than you say you do.'

'Her stage career was quite short, wasn't it?'

'From first to last, exactly three years.'

'I remember mother speaking of her. Mother admired her very much.'

'Yes, Guy, your mother would. Your mother is a very fine judge.'

'That's how I knew the face! Mother has a portrait of her—just a crayon—I've seen it.'

'Of course, Cecilia was long before your time, Guy. I was forgetting.'

'She threw up everything at the very height of her fame, didn't she?'

'Yes. London, Paris, New York, Vienna—all the capitals were at her feet.'

'But why? Did she marry?'

'No. She never married.'

'Was it illness? A break-down?'

'No . . . not illness . . . oh, this gives you no idea of her!'

'Why did she abandon her career, Raymond?'

'Would you really like to hear? Well, I've only told the story to very few people, and never before to a youngster like you, Guy, but I think perhaps you'll understand—you are 'simpatico', as she would have said—dear Cecilia—and you are going to be a priest soon, please God. She would have loved that. It's getting too dark to paint any more today, so I'll tell it to you now. Let's draw the curtains—that's better. Shall we sit in the firelight? No, you stay on the chesterfield. I'll take the basket-chair. Yes, I'd rather. I'm lazy and tired, and I want to stretch my legs. Just let me get my pipe going. There! Yes, that Swiss costume is the dress in which she sang Amina. Ah, she was a beautiful creature!

※

I first met Cecilia Bressan in Venice. I was a good many years young then—not so old as you are, Guy, and she was just a child, a little girl at the school of the good Sisters of the Stimmate.

I was mighty proud of having won an Art Scholarship, on the strength of which I had come to Venice to soak myself in Titian and Tintoretto. My father was no less pleased than myself at my success—though he took care not to let me know it *then*—and generous, but he believed that a walker in any business or profession should leave to make his own way. So there I was, not staying *en prince* in one of the huge hotels on the Grand Canal, but a boarder in a little native pension on the Zattere. How it all comes back to me! The tiny paved courtyard under my bedroom window, with oleanders in pots and flowering myrtle in great round tubs, whilst from the walls were hanging wicker cages full of songbirds, finches and canaries and linnets, and the old magpie who used to perch on the shoulder of Siora Eufemia, a sort of grandmother in the establishment, as she sat in the doorway as busy as one of the Fates with her eternal distaff. And the long room with the crowded tables in the *trattoria* where we used to dine so gaily, on lentil soup and wonderful fishes of the most delicious taste and unknown names, *risotto*, and stewed veal and pullets and cutlets and salads, washed down with good red wine of the Paduan district, and a glass of grappa or noyau as a treat. What Toscani and Sallas and Cavours we smoked! What mornings in the Scuola di San Rocco or among the Capaccios of the Schiavoni!

As you will have recognised by her family name—Bressan—Cecilia was a Venetian. My professors and various friends had furnished me in abundance with all sorts of letters of introduction in Venice, and there I made the acquaintance of Count Alvise Bressan, a patrician who had married an English wife—Cecily Brackenbury, in some remote fashion a cousin of my great aunt Brackenbury with whom I was a prime favourite. Aunt Brackenbury was an original, a friend of Balzac and George Sand. When she heard I was going to Venice the old lady insisted upon my calling at the Palazzo Bressan. She even wrote to her cousin, an attention which ensured me the friendliest reception.

The Contessa Bressan would, I think, have been called by our Irish friends a 'voteen'. Don't run away with the idea that she was a dull stupid fanatic. Nothing of the sort. I have met few more charming and cultured women.

Count Alvise had one passion in life—music. He patronised and was interested in all the arts it is true—he gave me, for example, much valuable advice and encouragement—but music was with him, to borrow a phrase of De Brosses, 'an inconceivable rage.' When he heard it, as Dr. Burney says of one of his forbears, he seemed 'to agonise with pleasure too great for the aching senses.' A close friend of Verdi, he had known Rossini, Donizetti, Auber. He was full of personal anecdote. Best of all he loved to talk of the old days of musical glory in Venice—to move in a world of dilettanti, professionals, virtuosi, choirmasters, soprani, opera-singers, teachers of counterpoint, a whole tuneful universe. He spoke of Scarlatti, Paisiello, Galuppi, of Guadagni and Farinelli, as though they were alive. He had a great stock of stories of delirious nights at the opera long ago—how at San Moise when Rosa Vitalba was singing in *Li rivali placati* flowers rained down from the galleries, whilst the stage was littered with sonnets to the favourite, printed in gold on rose-coloured silk, which came fluttering from the boxes, and even doves with little silver bells round their necks were let loose to wing their way to the songstress. He often used to tell with a chuckle how one day whilst officiating at the very altar, the Prete Rosso, suddenly inspired with a new musical conception and forgetful of the divine miracle which was about to take place through his hands, abruptly went off to the sacristy to jot down the notes on paper. And when the scatter-brained creature was hauled before the Holy Office for this sacrilege, he was acquitted!

I hope I am not doing that excellent man and devoted husband, Conte Alvise Bressan, an injustice when I say that he loved his wife even better for her superb voice. He was never tired of listening to her singing, and more than once I have heard him claim, 'Ah! The world has lost a great operatic star in the Contessa Bressan.' You can imagine his delight when he was informed by the Sisters of the Stimmate that Cecilia had certainly inherited her mother's talent.

It was the traditional custom at the Palazzo Bressan to give a fête for the Redentor, in mid-July you know. A reception was held in the evening followed by a ball, the whole suite of superb salons being thrown open for the occasion. That year was the first time that Cecilia, who was then (I suppose) about fifteen, had been allowed to be present. Her father, who was always ready to indulge her slightest wish, had persuaded the Contessa to permit her to attend for the earlier part of the evening any rate—her mother insisted that she should retire when dancing commenced—because, as he adroitly pleaded, the gala of the Redentor was no mere social and fashionable entertainment but a religious festival. All Venice was there, and it was with some difficulty that I made my way up the thronging staircase, through the press of silk and satin gowns, the tiaras and coronets, the violet soutanes and sashes, the orders, the dazzling uniforms.

The daughter of the house was very simply dressed in plain white muslin with quaint black mittens, her only ornament a few natural flowers. I can see her now in that brilliant assembly, a child, or little more than a child that she was, she looked more beautiful than any of the principesse and ambassadresses in the latest French creations and historic jewels. It so happened that I had been exchanging a word or two with her and was moving away when I heard a scream. By some chance—a window carelessly opened, a curtain billowing into the room—a lamp had been upset from a console, and her gown was ablaze. Snatching up a rug I wrapped it round the frightened child in an instant, and I am happy to say that, save for the shock and a few trifling burns, she was in a little while none the worse from what might have been the most serious of accidents. The thanks of her father and mother were literally unbounded. There is nothing which they would not have done to help, to further my interests—in fact, it was owing to their influence that several important commissions came my way, it was they who arranged and made a success of my first exhibition. They showed me a thousand kindnesses, and remained my staunchest, truest friends. To Cecilia I was her preserver, he who had saved her life.

Naturally, after I left Venice, for several years, I saw little of the Bressans. I always heard from Cecilia at Christmas, Easter and the Redemption, and I always remembered her festa, 22nd of November. I dined with the Contessa once or twice in London, when she was visiting her family here in England, and the last time she confided to me that her husband insisted upon Cecilia's voice being trained by the best professors. 'I think he would like her to become a professional opera-singer, Raymond,' she said. 'I know the Maestro Verdi urges it, but . . .' and she shook her head.

'Don't you wish it?' I asked.

'I don't know what to say . . . I acknowledge I am doubtful . . . the life of an opera-singer is difficult, very difficult . . . Of course I shall never go against my husband . . . Cecilia must decide for herself . . . A voice, a beautiful voice is after all one of God's gifts.'

'One of God's rarest and most precious gifts, dear Contessa.'

It was not so many months later that I heard of the death of my friend—*polmonite*. She had never been strong.

As the years went on I was carving out my own fortune—and time slips by . . . we are all terribly selfish, I fear . . . The Conte died whilst I was in America . . . but I will not detain you with all that.

I read in the papers with the rest of the world of Cecilia's Neapolitan début, how she sang Lucia at the Teatro San Carlo, and how the most critical of all audiences applauded her to the echo. Triumph followed triumph. Rome. Florence, Vienna, Paris, Milan . . . The virtuosi raved of her voice, her *soprano sfogato*, 'brilliant as a pearl', 'faultless and sweet', 'scattering a shower of silver melody', 'that voice which is itself a consolation'.

It was a morning in the last week of August—I remember I had just finished a portrait for a very influential sitter, an exceptionally difficult piece of work, and I was sitting there after breakfast cramming the dottles in my first morning's pipe—true economy, Guy my boy—and idly debating whether I should take a short holiday out of Town and where, when a note was brought me from the Hotel Splendide. Cecilia was in London, and would I lunch with her?

I had left a child—I found a woman, one of the loveliest women I have ever seen.

'And so my girl has turned into a famous prima donna?'

'Caro Raimondo, I hope I shall always be just a little girl to you. I have told them that I am to be denied to everybody, and now let us talk—and talk—and talk!'

When we spoke of her father and old times Cecilia began to cry a little, quite gently. 'You know,

Raimondo, that it is his wish, his dying wish, that I am obeying now.'

'How? In what way?'

'He made me promise that I would remain on the operatic stage at least three years. He said it would be a sin against art—against music—if the world were cheated of my voice. You know how he placed music before everything else. Well, eighteen months or rather more—one half of the three years—have passed——'

'But, Cecilia *mia*, aren't you happy on the stage? Happy in your glorious triumphs—your success?'

'I don't know what to say,' she replied, unconsciously echoing her mother's words. 'Sometimes I think I am. Sometimes I know I'm not.'

'Child, what is it you want?'

'I want rest—and quiet—and peace—and home. Above all—I want love!'

'Cecelia, the whole world loves you—the critics adore you!'

'Yes, Raimondo, that may all be true. But do they love the woman—or the voice? I want a better love than that.'

'I understand, dear.' And I kissed her on the forehead.

There was silence for a moment. Then the door opened, and there entered a maid, neat, pretty, and extremely self-possessed. In her hands she carried a large bunch of Maréchal Niel roses tied with yellow satin.

'What is it Bettina? Am I never to have a moment to myself? Did I not tell you most particularly that I was not to be disturbed?'

'Yes, madame,' answered the abigail in soft persuasive tones (too soft and too persuasive, I thought), 'but
these flowers——'

'They are lovely—and how sweet they smell!'
She replied burying her face in the roses. 'But they
could have waited.'

'There is also a note from Monsieur Lamoreux.'

'Did he send the flowers?'

'Yes, madam.'

'Here, take them . . . put them in water somewhere . . .'

'In your room, madame?'

'Where you like . . . no, not in my room . . . anywhere . . . take them yourself.'

'And the note, madame?'

'Lay it down there—on the writing-desk.'

'He asks for an answer, madame.'

'There is no answer. Say I am busy . . . engaged . . .
I have not time just now. And see that I'm not interrupted again until I ring.'

The name of André Lamoreux was familiar to me
as indeed it was to everybody else at the time. He was
acknowledged the leading tenor of the day. Not only
that, but all the women had fallen adoring on the new
Adonis, whilst all the men dressed after him for he had
as exquisite a taste in clothes as in mistresses. True, there
had been an ugly whisper or two touching his amours.
There was that tale of a schoolgirl in Berlin with whom
he was said to have been on very intimate terms, and
who poisoned herself in rather a horrible way. She had
left a letter (so it was rumoured) accusing him of the

most brutal cruelty, but has the world time to listen to the stuff hysterical girls write? Lord Castleraven, we all knew, had separated from his wife, but only some of us knew that a broken-hearted woman, refused the sight of her children, and to all intents an exile in Alnwick Castle, cursed the day she had seen the handsome face of André Lamoureux and listened to his lying honeyed tongue.

'I am opening at Covent Garden next season, Raimondo, and Monsieur Lamoreux sings with me.'

'What is your first role?'

'Amina. Monsieur Lamoreux is the Elvino. You'll be there?'

'Of course.'

Amina was one of Cecilia's favourite parts. The critics have remarked, and it is true, that she was fondest of Alice, the peasant maiden whose purity and love save her foster-brother Roberto from the fiend; Julia in Spontini's *La Vestale*; Ninetta, the slandered village girl. Paulina in *I Martiri*, I can never forget the fervour of her 'Io Cristiana!'; Miranda in *La Tempesta*; La Cenerentola. Some parts she disliked. Much as she admired *Fidelio* she scrupled to doing Leonora because she had to wear a boy's costume—you have seen my sketch of her—she would not sing it more than half a dozen times in all. Violetta she absolutely declined in spite of more than one impresario, backed too by a hint from someone in very high places, and the suggestion of the Maestro himself.

'You don't like André Lamoreux, *carina*?'

'No, Raimondo. He repels me . . . Oh, yes, I know he is the handsomest man on the stage, at least that's what people say. And his voice, of course, his voice is wonderful. A supreme artist. Have you heard his Jean in *Le Prophète*? No? It is marvellous. And yet with it all, Raimondo, I cannot like him—nor his gifts.'

'Poor flowers!'

'Yes—they are lovely roses—look at the yellows—but somehow I cannot like them coming from him. He seems to taint everything he touches—I would rather have a bunch of snowdrops or primroses from—oh!'

'From whom?'

'Oh, nobody, Raimondo,' and she bent her head covered with blushes.

'Come, come, Cecilia, *figliuola mia*, I'm your old *cugino*—old *compare* Raimondo. Now tell me all about it. Come, confess, my child.'

'Well, Raimondo . . . I am in love.'

'Bene—benissimo, my child . . . I mean that's as may be. With whom?'

'Oh! I can't . . .'

'Yes . . . yes . . . yes . . . come along. Is it anyone I know?'

'I think not. He's quite undistinguished.'

'And poor?'

'I never thought of it. I have plenty for both.'

'Tell me, who is he?'

'Have you ever heard of Maurice O'Donnell?'

'No . . . never . . . he sounds Irish . . . very Irish.'

'He is Irish . . . he sings . . . baritone . . . only small parts . . . but—he sang one season at the Crisosforno—

Father said his baritone was one of the fullest and sweetest he had ever heard.'

'Yes? Well, your father certainly knew.'

'And then he dined with us—and mother liked him—he had an aunt who was a nun—a Dominican— and I used to meet him coming from early Mass at San Giobbe . . . and . . .'

'San Giobbe . . . down in Cannaregio, if I remember my Venice right . . . a fair step from the Palazzo Bressan.'

'Anyway, we used to go to Mass there . . . and . . . and . . .'

'Does he love you, *cara*? But what a silly question to ask. Of course, he must.'

'Well, he says he does . . . oh, yes, I know he does . . .'

'He's a very lucky man, dear. You'll allow an old friend to say that—a very lucky man. I hope you will both be very—very happy'.

'Now, Raimondo, you understand why I want— why I intend to leave the stage.'

'I understand.'

'After this season—there are eight weeks in New York—and then one more season in Paris and then the last!'

I believe critics still talk—or write—of La Bressan in *La sonnambula*. There is a tendency today to sneer *sotto voce* at Bellini, who was far freer than your modern composers—but nowadays like everything else music seems to have gone to the devil! However, Guy, you don't want to be bored with an old man's views and outpourings upon music . . . If Amine as sung by

Cecilia Bressan was not the highest achievement of art I don't know what was.

I was there in my stall the first night. God! I shall never forget the enthusiasm. She was called again and again. And Lamoreux as Elvino. The fellow was handsome—deucedly handsome—and he could sing! O'Donnell? Oh, yes, he sung some Swiss peasant . . . how does it go? 'In Elvezia non v'ha rosa . . .' and jolly good he was!

Well, I saw a lot of Cecilia that autumn. And I was introduced to O'Donnell. A regular gossoon. Blue-grey eyes, black hair, and a mystic with the blarney on his tongue. But that boy loved Cecilia . . . yes, that was plain enough . . . he loved her, and he would have loved her had she been a lodging house drab instead of the world's prima dona. He was mettle through and through was Maurice O'Donnell.

André Lamoreux loved her too—in his fashion. He had often boasted that no woman could resist him, and if goodwife gossip spoke true there was reason for his boast.

That winter I saw quite a deal of both of O'Donnell and Lamoreux. Maurice and I became great friends. As to Lamoreux—the fellow was always polite enough, in fact when he knew how Cecilia regarded me he went out of his way to cultivate my acquaintance—lunches, suppers, parties at Richmond and so forth—but as to Lamoreux I never could like him. He wanted to marry Cecilia—he had proposed to her twice—and he waited. Naturally in the course of their work they were constantly thrown together. Outside the theatre she avoided him. I often made a third, on nights she was not singing, with Cecilia and Maurice in some Soho restaurant. She preferred the Chanticleer or Gennaro or the Petit Riche to all the gilt and glamour of West End luxury. In Soho she felt, as she used to say, among her own people.

It was not until Christmas that the engagement of Maurice and Cecilia became public property, and following upon that flashed the news that she intended to retire from the stage in a twelvemonth's time. Society gasped; the critics wailed; managers in England, in Italy, in Germany, in America lamented in polyglot chorus.

'Merely a ruse to send up the price of the stalls!' sneered Lady Talgarth.

'And a deuced sight more smart than having your jewels stolen,' added Sir Frank Guisley.

Before long, however, the world woke to the fact that Cecilia's retirement was not a clever advertisement but was indubitably and deliberately predetermined and resolved.

How happy she was in those days—how supremely happy! 'I've kept my word,' she said. 'Father must be satisfied now. I have made my choice. And in one short year I shall win my release.'

'Your release, *cara*?'

'Yes, from the artificiality, and the hollowness and tawdriness of it all!'

'Yet you are depriving the world of much.'

'Has the world any right to stand between me and my happiness?'

It was at a small party on the Befana that Cecilia told us the news of her engagement. True, I had been privileged to know before, but it was quite simply done. There were about a dozen of us present in her suite at the Splendide when she took Maurice's thin hand and said: 'This is the man whom I am going to marry. I shall leave the stage in a year. Please congratulate me.' André Lamoreux, who was there, did not move a muscle of his face, but his eyes glinted. His manner was perfect as always when he bowed to her and said without a tremor in his voice: 'Signorina, we do congratulate you. Signor Maurizio is fortunate indeed.' I think Cecilia liked him then better than ever before.

What Tagliafico and Herr Schodel said I will not attempt to describe. They raved; they stamped and danced and tore their hair. They swore; they argued; they entreated; they wept. All in vain. Their only consolation was in hurrying forward the projected revival of Mercuniali's *I Capuleti e i Montecchi*, preparations for which had already begun on an imposing scale. They made her sign a contract for twelve performances. You don't know the opera? I suppose not. It's a difficult piece to mount, they tell me, and costly. There is the masquerade scene in Act I, for example, and only the purest soprano can sing Giulietta. The librettist has kept pretty close to Shakespeare, which is in his favour, and much of the recitative is nothing else than a clever rendition of *Romeo and Juliet*. Cecilia was the Giulietta, of course; Lamoreux, Romeo; and Maurice il conte Parigi. You will remember that in the last act, Juliet's monument, Parigi has his song 'Soave fior, con angeli *esaltata* . . .' Oh! I forgot! Of course you've never heard it. How should you? Anyway, the book follows the play quite closely. In Act III Juliet is lying apparently dead in her tomb and Paris enters to scatter flowers over her and perform 'true love's rite'. Romeo rushes forward, and there is a duel in which Paris falls. I designed Cecilia's dresses. Blue brocade and cloth of gold for Act I—I copied it from Veronese—you remember the poet's lines:

> in that gorgeous dress of beaten gold
> Which is more golden than the golden sun
> No woman Veronese looked upon
> Was half so fair as thou

—and then a simple white robe.

I Capuleti e i Montecchi succeeded almost beyond all expectation. Her admirers said that Cecilia had never sung so divinely as in Giulietta, and Lamoreux was certainly the ideal Romeo. It was chosen as the last performance of the season, the last time Cecilia would sing at Covent Garden.

The house was packed. Almost half-an-hour before the overture I went round to Cecilia's dressing-room, and was surprised to find her unhappy and unwell. 'Raimondo,' she said, 'I am full of fear for tonight.'

'Why, my dear, have a migraine? You look strangely pale. Are you overtired? Your voice?'

'No. But I am afraid. Something is going to happen to me . . . oh! It's only a *crise de nerfs*, I expect . . . you will come round after, Raimondo? And then we will have supper together quietly, you and I and Maurice. If only tonight were over!'

It was remarked that André Lamoreux appeared in even better voice than usual that evening. There was something tenderer in his great love duet; some note of triumph seemed to swell in the aria when he proclaimed his nuptials with Juliet.

The curtain rose on the last act. There was the churchyard. Tall yews dark and sombre pierced the starlit sky. In the Gothic tomb, an elaborate structure all pinnacles and crockets, lay Cecilia in her white robe, her hair hanging negligently loose, upon the bier covered with its heavy pall of black velvet. Maurice entered; he stood a moment gazing upon her;—I think they smiled at one another—and then began his song 'Soave fior . . . soave fior . . .' As the last notes died away, lithe as a panther and with a panther's agile grace Romeo leaped on to the stage. There was the quick parley, the challenge and swords flashed. Both were expert fencers. Paris fell. Romeo broke into song: 'Giulietta! caro nome . . .' Suddenly there was a piercing scream. Cecilia struggled to her feet. Scream followed scream. The orchestra stopped in confusion. Her face as white as paper, her eyes almost starting from her head, she pointed to the body lying on the stage. Blood was welling from the white satin doublet—blood and blood and more blood!

Maurice's blue-grey eyes were closed—those eyes which always reminded me of the wide Atlantic and his native Galway—closed never to open again.

André Lamoreux stood as if stunned. The curtain fell like lightning. There was the coroner's quest. A foil had been supplied somehow minus the button. Who was to blame? Certainly not Monsieur Lamoreux who was—the papers said—heart-broken at having killed a fellow artist. The coroner entirely exonerated him, was sympathetic and condoled; whilst the jury added to their verdict of accidental death to the effect that all weapons used on the stage ought to be carefully blunted, and immovable buttons affixed to all rapiers and foils.

Cecilia? Well, my dear Guy, I won't talk about that. I was (I believe) the only one save the doctor and the priest privileged to see her during that summer—that dreadful summer—poor little wan white widowed soul, always dressed in mourning.

The managerial syndicate, Tagliafico and Herr Schodel behaved with the utmost courtesy. But she insisted—that was Cecilia all over—she said to me: 'Raimondo, the time I promised my father is not yet expired. I am bound to him and I have my duty to my public. I am a servant of the public for another eight months, and then my life is my own.'

And so that winter she sung at the Metropolitan— Lucia, Amina, Amalia, Alice . . .

Next spring she was in Paris, and I went over from London to see her.

'Raimondo, *caro* Raimondo, you will come to my last night, won't you?'

'Cecilia, dear, listen. Have you quite decided to leave the stage? Don't you think in view of what has happened you might be well advised——'

'*Caro*, my plans are made.'

183

'But, my dear, have you considered? If you dislike the theatre—opera—there is the great platform—oratorios—sacred music.'

'*Caro*, my plans are made.'

'What are they?'

'I have told nobody, dear. But you shall be the first to know.'

And with that I was content.

The last night—positively the last night—upon which Cecilia Bressan was to appear drew the whole musical world to Paris. The opera chosen was—will you be surprised to hear it?—*I Capuleti e i Montecchi.* André Lamoreux was the Romeo. At first she protested. 'Liebchen,' said Schodel, 'where are we to find another Romeo? And it is only this once—and the last time. After all, it was an accident—a most unfortunate, unhappy accident—but the public, whose servants we are, *they* insist. Where are we to find another Romeo?'

Cecilia went through rehearsals like a statue. I saw her shudder once whilst Romeo clasped her in his arms as the script directs. He smiled. I was present in the wings at the final *répétition*. When Lamoreux came off I heard one of his pals say:

'*Mon brave*, she's just a bit of ice or marble.'

'If ice, I'll melt her, you'll see,' was the laughing response. 'If marble, I've given one stroke with the chisel already—eh?'

The last night—well, you can imagine it. The Grand Opera packed to suffocation. All Paris—all the musical world, London, New York, Milan, Naples, Vienna, in front. Women were sobbing, and men—yes, men broke down and cried like children as she sang.

The curtain slowly ascended for the final act. Upon the catafalque—very French and very ornamental—lay Cecilia. Il conte Parigi came on stage. I half started to my feet in my stall. It was Maurice! Was I mad? Was I dreaming?

And then his voice—Maurice's voice rang through the house. 'Soave fior . . . soave fior!' Cecilia rose and opened her eyes . . . she held wide her arms . . . oh, this was all wrong! The man next to me fidgeted in his place and muttered something. Romeo leaped upon the stage. Blades were drawn. They crossed. And then beneath the powder and the paint his face blanched with fear. He glanced this way and that in mortal terror. But his opponent pressed him hard. The sword flew from his hand, and as he stood there gibbering and clawing at the air Parigi passed the lithe thin rapier through his body, turned and went off by the wings.

The house was in an uproar. The curtain was lowered. A couple of doctors hastily summoned from the boxes made their way on to the stage where André Lamoreux lay dead, his face frozen with a horror it is not good to look upon. 'Heart failure . . . a sudden seizure' was the pronouncement. There was no trace of a wound. And yet as had all seen——

What of Salvaggi, you will ask, who was billed to sing il conte Parigi? Salvaggi was in his dressing room chatting with two or three friends. He had not been called for the last act, and he had no idea it had begun. On a night like that such mistakes were excusable. And the call-boy? When he was running up to Salvaggi's room he had met il conte Parigi on the stairs who said: 'All right! I'm going down now! I'm ready for the stage.'

Cecilia summed up the whole thing to me. 'He murdered Maurice—he killed him deliberately. And so Maurice came back that night!'

What do I think, Guy? I don't know what to think. Put some more coal on the fire, old boy, it's getting low.

It was about a fortnight later that Raymond Henderson asked rather abruptly if I would go with him to St. Anthony's, Kensington. We had just finished lunch, and were sitting over cigarettes and coffee.

'It will be time if we get there by half-past three,' he said. 'Do you know it?'

I confessed I did not.

'It's quite a small place. Actually the chapel to the Convent of Poor Clares.'

And that afternoon I knelt by his side in the curious unearthly church. Vespers finished, and as we entered we heard from the pulpit a brown friar thundering against the modernism of the age and exalting the mystery of the Incarnation. He ceased, kissed the purple stole that hung around his neck and disappeared from view. Already a server was transforming the high altar into a blaze of light. The jubilant organ burst forth, the sandaled priest in his cope of ivory satin passed from the sacristy to the altar, where he sanctified and unveiled the tabernacle. As the thurible was wafted towards that great gilt star and the heavy clouds of incense began to fill the air there sounded from behind the curtained grille the strains of the litany of Loreto—that perfect litany—sung by those women who were enshrined there dead to the world.

Salus infirmorum,
Refugium Peccatorum,
Consolatrix afflictorum, Ora . . . ora pro nobis.

Consoler of the afflicted . . . pray, pray for us!
And so on through the chants of that exquisite hymn, calling upon Mary by Her sweetest dearest names, until the priest intoned:

Ona pro nobis sancta Dei Genitrix!

And the nuns from Tribune answered:

Ut digni efficiama promissionibus Christi.

Above the rest there rose a voice of marvellous sweetness and power, which thrilled me as I kneeled there and drank it in.

And I thought of all the tales I had heard of the Order, the most austere the Church knows. I thought of their absolute enclosure, a veritable entombment; the dark veil; how they walk barefoot, clad in the roughest coarsest clothes; the perpetual fast; the vigils; the broken sleep; utter renunciation and the abject poverty.

Raymond's face was grave and as we passed out into the street. He took me by the arm.

'Now, Guy,' he whispered, 'now you can say you have heard Cecilia Bressan.'

The Man on the Stairs

The very air rests thick and heavily
Where murder has been done.
—Joanna Baillie

'DAMNED nonsense.'

'Oh well, of course, Fanshawe, if you are going to take it like that——'

'And how else can any sensible man take it? Come now, Hatton,' continued the exceedingly rubicund and ruffled Mr. James Fanshawe, beating a sharp tattoo upon the table, 'try to put yourself in my position. Yes, yes,' anticipating an argumentative interruption, for Mr. Fanshawe was a gentleman who, even as his best friends allowed, loved to hear himself and no one else talk, whilst his enemies used to compare him to Tennyson's brook, 'yes, yes, my dear fellow, we all know that you are simply crazy on spooks and table-turning and Sir Oliver Lodge and Conan Doyle, who wrote very sensible stories by the way until he took up this planchette business—Sherlock Holmes was quite good—but here I am, I have just bought a splendid old place, incidentally I should have thought it would have appealed to you, yet when I ask you to come down for the inside of a week or so you put me off with some fantastic yarn about Cheriton Manor being haunted and dangerous and—poof!' Mr. Fanshawe crushed the stub of his cigarette in the ash tray, and finished off his whisky and soda with the air of dousing a tiresome discussion.

The time was about two-thirty on a late October afternoon. The scene, the smoking room of a well-known London club. In distant corners half-a-dozen members who had strolled in replete from lunch were lazily reading the papers until they fell asleep or found something better to do. Mr. Fanshawe, a natty well-paunched gentleman—one could never think of him under any other designation in his late fifties, who looked like a retired city man, as indeed he was, amply filled a most comfortable armchair in a most comfortable corner in a window whence he could see all St. James Street wag by and benignly approve. Just then his usual placidity, perhaps rather a surface quality with him after all, was undeniably perturbed, and although he strove hard to keep his temper there appeared more than one sign of an imminent explosion. His friend Hatton, tall, angular and wiry, seemed of a different calibre, and at the moment there was an expression of earnestness upon his tired, lined face which gave it a shade of almost monkish melancholy, as he leaned forward to give more weight to his words.

'I know, Fanshawe, I know. Of course it is bound to be a most terrible disappointment——'

'It's not a disappointment at all.'

'But I am sure that after what I tell you, you will see the wisdom, the necessity, for leaving Cheriton during the winter months at all events.'

'And why during the winter months?'

'Because then the manifestations are at their worst.'

'Manifestations! Really, Hatton, if we were not such old friends—How can you talk such infernal rubbish!'

'Infernal, yes, that is just what they are, only unfortunately not rubbish.'

'Do you actually mean to tell me you believe in all this rot of blue lights and clanking chains and that sort of stuff?'

'James, by everything that I hold sacred it is true.' His voice shook slightly, and he spoke in low eager tones. The other voice seemed to gather loudness and vexation in reply.

'What is true? You haven't told me anything definite yet. Only vague warnings—it never does for a prophet to be too exact, I know. What does it all amount to? And let me tell you, John,' with a sudden fierce crackle of irritation, 'and take it as you will, I call it damned bad taste, yes, bad taste, when we meet for the first time after nearly two years and I ask you down to my new place, just for a house-warming among old friends, to come out with all this preposterous nonsense like a regular death's head at the feast. It's not as though I believed in it, mind you. I don't care twopence halfpenny for all your spiritualism and crystal gazing, and you know jolly well that I don't. Yet there are some crazy fools about. At any rate, if

190

you won't put your legs under my mahogany, there are others who will.'

'I wish you wouldn't take it so hardly. If you will only listen to me quietly for a few moments I am sure I can make you see——'

'Listen to you quietly! What on earth else have I been doing this past hour and a half?' Mr. Fanshawe found it convenient to forget his own not inconsiderable share in the conversation. 'As soon as I told you during lunch that I had bought Cheriton Manor you began, and you've kept on about it ever since.'

'I only wish I had been in England, James, when you took up the idea of Cheriton, for then——'

'It would have been all the same if you had. Not counting what I gave for it I have spent more than two thousand on the house from first to last, for it was in a shocking state of neglect—it had to be modernised right and left. It took a deuce of a time too and now I have got it ship-shape I am not going to be put off by any hanky-panky spiritualism. So that's that.'

'I only wonder at the Dormers caring for it to go out of the family. I remember Lady Anne Dormer. But then she was an old, old woman when I was quite a small boy. Even she used to spend the late autumn and winter on the Riviera each year. She said it was health. My father said she couldn't get the servants to stay in the house during the dark months.'

'There you go again. It's too bad. Do try to be sensible. Now look here, won't you really come down to Cheriton next week as I ask you?'

'I'd rather not.'

'What am I to understand by that? You seem to have arrived back home after all this time in a deuce of a funny mood anyhow. Are you going to drop all your old friends?'

'Don't say that. It hurts. If it were anywhere else, James, but to Cheriton, I would come to stay with you like a shot, and for as long as you liked.'

'Well, I am bound to say you seemed ready enough until I mentioned Cheriton Manor. Can't you see that it is all moonshine, this spook business? Take any old house such as Cheriton wherever you like in town or country, preferably in the country, a place that for some quite good reason or the other has been shut up for years just as Cheriton has been—family can't keep it going, death duties, taxes, younger generation prefer to live in town, want excitement, it's all excitement now-a-days—and what, I ask you, is the result? Tales are bound to get round: a deserted house, mystery, haunt-ed—boh! I hate the very word. We aren't living in the Middle Ages, although upon my soul I begin to think we must be. Apparently sensible level-headed men and women are quite cracked on this one subject. I suppose some of your modern up-to-date doctors could explain it—aftermath of the war, crowd neurasthenia—but I am wandering from the point. You accepted my invita-tion, John. A plain answer to a plain question. Are you going to back out?'

'I would rather not—I cannot stay at Cheriton Manor. You can't know the place and its reputation as well as I do. Don't forget that my old father was rector of Canons Roothing only seven miles away, and I lived there until I went up to King's. I am not talking at random. Believe me, James, I hate to offend you, and I know that I am offending you—oh yes, I am—more than you yourself are really aware of perhaps.'

'Well, if you want it quite straight, I *am* annoyed, and I think I have a perfect right to be thoroughly annoyed. I won't disguise it from you. So you aren't coming? Yes or no.'

'I would rather not.'

'That is to say, no.' Fanshawe rose to his feet, and with an unmistakable sneer added, 'You're afraid.'

The other without moving from his chair lifted his eyes and looked his friend straight in the face. 'Yes, there are some things of which I am afraid,' he said quietly. 'Let me tell you——'

'Oh, no, thanks,' interrupted Fanshawe with a harsh laugh his already high colour rising a little more, 'I don't want to hear the yarn—keep it for the next Christmas annual. Tell it at the next séance you attend, the circle or whatever they call the mumbo-jumbo now.' His voice rose higher, and more than one member in their vicinity looked up for a moment from his paper. 'But don't let me hear any more of this rubbish, and for heaven's sake try to cultivate a little common sense. Let me tell you one thing, and I am quite serious about it, I'll give you or any other fellow who can show me a ghost in Cheriton Manor a hundred pounds down for each bogie he raises. There, that's a firm offer, and a pretty safe one too, I'll wager. Ghosts, psha!' And then in a slightly smoother tone as he was moving towards the door he greeted a new-comer with a nod, 'Afternoon, Markham, going to keep fine? I think so.'

Hatton followed him for a moment with his eyes, and leaning back sighed heavily. 'My word, Hatton, old Fanshawe seems fairly put out about something. What's stung him now? And what's all this about a hundred pounds? I couldn't help hearing if the old buffer will raise his voice for the benefit of the whole smoking-room . . . well.'

'Nothing much, Markham. We were only having a little discussion and Fanshawe can't bear to be contradicted.'

'I know, any more than he can bear to lose at bridge. Well, I hope he recovers his temper by Friday anyway, because I am motoring down to this new place of his, new old place I ought to call it, for by all accounts Cheriton Manor is as ancient as the hills and a little bit over.'

'You are going down to Cheriton on Friday?'

'Yes, do you know it? Fanshawe has only just settled in, and mighty proud he seems of his new toy. According to what he says the place was in a shocking state when he found it. However, I've no qualms, I assure you. He knows how to make himself jolly comfortable, and his guests too, I will say that.'

'It was what I was telling him about Cheriton Manor that rather upset him, I'm afraid.'

'You know Cheriton then? And what is it like?' queried Markham, lighting a cigarette. 'All gables and black and white? What were you heckling him about anyway? Drains?'

'No. I think perhaps I ought to tell you since you are going to stay there.'

'Don't run away with the idea that Fanshawe does anything but patronize a poor younger son who can hardly make two ends meet. I am under no illusions, and I know very well why I am being asked down to Cheriton. Bridge, Hatton, bridge. I can play a pretty good hand, and there's nothing the old boy loves better than his four after dinner. He says my play suits his. In plain words I have to do all the work, for he's not above making a pretty foul bloomer now and again, and I just sit mum and say nothing but "Bad luck that, sir, bad luck."'

'You may laugh and joke just as he did. I can't help that. Since you are an invited guest it is my duty to tell you that Cheriton Manor is haunted—horribly haunted.'

'Oh, how awfully interesting.' And Markham dropped into a chair. 'But I say, you surely never let on to Fanshawe that there was a ghost, did you?'

'I warned him, as I am warning you now.'

'Whew! That's torn it then. Cheriton Manor is the apple of the old man's eye, and you know what he thinks about ghosts.'

'There certainly is a ghost, and a very fearful and malignant ghost.'

'Of course I can't pretend to know much about that sort of thing. I met a man once who went in for table-turning and crystal-gazing a lot, but I've never come up against it personally.'

'Do you know who are going to Cheriton besides yourself?' asked Hatton.

'Fanshawe was talking about quite a small party, only four, I expect for one bridge table. The real house-warming—the royal beano—will be later on, in December, I understand; this is only a preliminary canter.'

'Could you possibly find out for me, then, who are going to be your fellow guests?'

'No, I don't very well see how I could manage that. I can't ask the old chap point-blank, can I? But why do you want to know?' he curiously queried.

'Because I should warn them too, just as I warned my old friend, and as I am going to warn you.'

Markham relieved his feelings and his frank surprise by a soft whistle. Then, with a glance at the elder man, he said in a voice that was just a thought too obviously careless, 'Oh, that'll be all right as far as I am concerned. Of course I'm glad to know and all that sort of thing, because if I hear the regulation footsteps in the corridor I certainly shan't bother to get out of bed. But you can trust me to look after myself.'

'Then you are a sceptic too,' said Hatton gravely.

'Oh, I wouldn't go as far as that. I daresay there's a lot of truth in what that chap says somewhere "There are more things in Heaven and earth," but I simply don't let it worry me.'

'To you, Markham, I may seem an old fool, a silly crank. But I want you to listen to me for a bit. I have travelled in many countries and seen many strange things. I have some knowledge, some slight knowledge, of what we conveniently call the occult. There are forces, terrible forces of darkness and power, who can and do manifest themselves. For some reason, be it what it may, there is a concentration of these forces at Cheriton Manor. The family history of the Dormers—they are all dead now and one can speak freely—is simply damnable. For centuries they have been a legend throughout the countryside. The men were rakes and duellists and murderers, and if report says true, something worse. The women were wantons and witches, wholly evil. A bad, bad stock. Cheriton was originally a religious house, and under Henry VIII, Geoffrey Dormer, one of Cromwell's men, stabbed a monk at the altar as he was saying mass. His blood flowed into the chalice, and as he fell dying he cursed his slayers. They hanged the last abbot to an oak opposite his own church door. And Dormer got Cheriton as a reward for his zeal in the King's service. A Dormer was the wildest spirit of the Hell Fire Club at Medmenham. Buck Dormer was infamous even in Regency days. I remember his son's wife, Lady Anne. She was the toast of the gay Victorians. The tale went that she sold herself to the devil for a pretty face. I used to see her, a raddled and wrinkled hag, and she was always glancing back over her left shoulder and clutching her companion, for she could never be left alone. The villagers said that she was looking to see when old Scratch would come to claim his bargain.'

'And which of these interesting—er—gentlefolk revisits his ancestral halls?'

'Black Dormer. He made his own sister his mistress, and when she was to be married to a neighbouring squire upon the wedding eve he cut her throat. They used to show the room where she was killed. A gloomy place enough. It opens on to the gallery at the top of the great stairs, and at midnight he walks down stairs, and in his hand his sword. Sometimes the blade is clean, but if there is blood upon the sword those who see him die within the year. He lived in the days of Charles I, and his portrait painted by Vandyke was one of the show pieces of the Manor. I expect it is in America now.'

'Yes, but I imagine that even then you could hardly murder your relations promiscuously and get away with it. How did he escape?'

'It was supposed that the unfortunate bride was assassinated by thieves who had broken in on account of the family jewels, the pearls and diamonds she was to wear next day at the altar. The truth was only known when, half a century after, Dormer confessed it on his death-bed.'

'But how about the family when they lived there? Did none of them ever see him?'

'More than once. There is an old saying though, "A Dormer never hurt a Dormer yet," and they felt safe enough. Black Dormer: I remember the Vandyke well. He was a handsome fellow with his blue eyes and flowing hair. They only called him Black because his deeds were black, and his heart was black, black as hell.'

'Does Fanshawe know all these bright spots of family history?'

'I can't tell. He would not listen to me, but I hope what I say will not be lost upon you, at any rate. Don't go to Cheriton Manor.'

'We seem in for a pretty lively time. After all, this black gentleman may not take it into his head to walk while we are there.'

'You do not believe, I see. I have done my best. You don't believe any more than my old friend believed when he laughed in my face and offered a hundred pounds to the man who would show him a ghost in Cheriton Manor.' John Hatton rose wearily. He was looking very old and tired. 'I have no more to say, Markham. My last word is, don't go to Cheriton Manor.'

Cyril Markham watched him with a puzzled expression. 'Queer old bird,' he thought. 'I wonder how much of this ghost business he really believes. I'd forgotten for the moment, of course he's a Catholic, and so naturally he swallows anything. Let him yarn till all is blue, it'll take more than the spook of a gentleman who was a gay dog when Charles I walked and talked to keep me away from Fanshawe's port and his bridge, with the chance of making a bit. If one could only get hold of that hundred quid now . . .' He smoked a cigarette meditatively, when suddenly throwing it aside he made his way to the telephone booth in the club hall. 'Primrose 0202.'

About an hour or rather more later Cyril Markham was in the sitting-room of a small flat in the Finchley Road direction engaged in close conclave with his companion, a young man of six and twenty. Tall, undeniably handsome, he betrayed his profession by all those indefinable but unmistakable characteristics which stamp the actor. At the moment he was giving such close attention to the discussion under weigh that he actually forgot to sip his whisky and soda for quite ten minutes together.

"Let's get it clear from the beginning at any rate,' he was saying in a singularly musical voice. 'You are going down on Friday to this jolly old house which is jolly well haunted. The chap who owns it has betted a hundred of the best that nobody can show him the ghost, and you are proposing to meet his wishes in the shape of my humble self on a basis of fifty-fifty.'

'You've got it slick. Now——'

'But, my dear fellow, the whole thing simply bristles with snags. I can't see on earth how we could work it. It sounds all right, but——'

'Isn't it worth a little trouble for fifty?'

'It's worth a damned lot of trouble. I could do very well with five, let alone fifty, just now. I was never so bloody hard up in my life.'

'Well then, listen to me, and don't be a fool. I've planned it all out top-hole. The ghost apparently stalks downstairs at midnight from a bedroom which opens out on to a gallery overlooking the hall. I know that Fanshawe is mighty proud of this hall—it is one of the features of the place, and it won't need much suggesting on my part to get him to arrange the bridge-table there. What you have to do it really very simple. In the first place, you must have a cavalier costume and a sword. There's not any difficulty about that I suppose?'

'Oh no, Isaacs or Johnny Beecher will have the clothes all right.'

'What about those togs you wore in "Strafford"? That was a first-rate make-up, and all you have to do is to walk down the stairs at twelve o'clock."

'In another man's house. I don't half like it. I shall feel no end of a fool. Suppose he twigs?'

'Not he! I can feed him during the evening with a hint or two and a mysterious story. You know the kind of thing . . . Of course I don't believe in ghosts myself, but a funny thing happened to a cousin of mine . . .'

'Take care that a funny thing doesn't happen to a friend of yours.' The young actor still hesitated. He looked gloomily at the lighted end of his cigarette. 'How am I to get into the place anyhow?' he queried. 'I'm not going to do any climbing through a window tricks or cat-burglar stunts. The local bobby is always mouthing round these big places in the country. Nothing else to do I s'pose. I knew there would be a crab somewhere.'

'Oh, do listen, I've got it all mapped out,' interrupted the other. 'I'm driving down on Friday, and you can come along with me as my chauffeur-valet. We'll take the togs with us in an extra suitcase, and during the evening you can easily slip up to my bedroom and change there, and just lie doggo until twelve o'clock when you do the cavalier act. It's simple as paint.'

'It sounds damned risky to me.'

'Of course there's a certain amount of risk. That's half the fun, isn't it? We can scout round on Saturday, you and I, and see the best way of working it. There's sure to be some room off the hall with French windows so you can step out when we've all had our big fright. And look here, if you don't like the lie of the land we'll just cry the whole thing off. But are you game if it can be worked?'

'Yes, I suppose so,' was the somewhat unenthusiastic reply. 'But if the old chap finds out and cuts up rough——'

'He won't, I tell you,' interrupted Markham, 'and if he does stand the racket. What can he say or do? Only curse and swear a bit. He'd never give himself away by raising a dust. But you'll have to put some pep into it, Claude, no half-and-half business. After all, it will only be like acting in some bally old period film.'

Claude Heseltine mixed himself another whisky and soda, a very amber-coloured fluid this time. When he had gulped down half his glass the scene wore a distinctly brighter aspect. After all what a glorious rag it would be! And fifty quid for it as well! At worst, as Markham said, the old chap daren't cut up too rough, surely. He wouldn't want to show himself up as an utter ass. Then later perhaps a par or two might be worked in the press. He knew that costume parts were his real line. A par with just a hint from Mrs. Rumour might lead to a decent shop in town. Another drink, and things began to look even more roseate. 'By Jove, Cyril, I believe there's something in it after all.'

'Something in it, of course there's something in it. Fifty quid for you and fifty for me. It's just as easy as easy. Now look here . . .' and they settled down to talk.

Since Cheriton Manor has been illustrated in *Rural Life*, although it was a good while ago, I believe, I do not propose to attempt any description of the house, which in every respect justified the agents' *cliché* 'a Tudor gem.' As you motor along the rather solitary main road you find yourself echoing the phrase in all sincerity when you catch a glimpse through the trees of the gables and the famous twisted chimney-stacks. It is an ideal spot, a trifle remote perhaps, even a trifle too picturesque to seem quite real, Neither Cyril Markham nor his ultra-smart young chauffeur were by any means impression-able and their minds were undoubtedly pre-occupied with something other than aesthetic appreciation, yet even from the curt remarks they exchanged as after the forty miles run the Riley turned in at the old lodge gates, and the Manor came more and more fully in sight from behind the autumn-tinted leafery, it was plain they were both moved to an unusual admiration. Over and above his elegant blarney there was indeed a note of sincerity in the congratulations with which Markham greeted his host. 'By Jove, sir, you've got a ripping place down here. I don't know when I've seen such a house. By gad, it's top-hole.'

Mr. Fanshawe, very accurately dressed to play the rôle of country squire but yet having the air of not be-ing quite at home in his sports-jacket and tweeds, had met him in the porch and listened with obvious grati-fication. With manly chest expanding like a pouter-pigeon, he replied just a shade too casually, 'Yes, my dear fellow, I think that without boasting I may claim that Cheriton Manor has features—distinct features. I'm glad you're here fairly early because I can show you round a bit. The others—you've met them both, Garraway and Peter Prothero—can't join us until just in time for dinner. They're coming along together. But, God bless my soul! I am forgetting my duties. What do you say to a cup of tea, or perhaps something stronger after your run, eh? And then a wash, and tea when you come down.' Markham acknowledged that at the moment the 'something stronger' certainly seemed to meet the situation. By this time they had reached the inner hall, the centre of the house, and if he was eulogistic when his host welcomed him, he waxed positively enthusiastic as he gazed around. The hall was indeed well worthy of all praise, Large and lofty, it was panelled in oak black with age, and vaulted with huge black rafters. In the wide open fire-place a great pile of logs blazed cheerily up the huge gaping chimney. Opposite, an oak staircase of exceptional width and stateliness, flanked at the foot with two great demi-wyverns, supporters of shields bearing the Dormer arms and motto *Gare à qui nous touche*, led up to a wide gallery which ran along the whole length of one side, branching off into corridors right and left. There were some three or four doors, giving on to the gallery, and as with his back to the fire he basked in its generous warmth and sipped his drink 'in mighty content,' he saw his valet preceded by a footman who was carrying a medley of suitcases and, rugs appear 'above', as old plays have it, and pass through a centre door into the room beyond.

'Ah, yes, Markham,' said his host following his guest's eyes, 'I've put you in one of those rooms up there. The oldest part of the house, and not the least comfortable. Since there are only three of you I thought it might be more convenient, at least my housekeeper Mrs. Baxter suggested the arrangement.'

'I am sure I shall be perfectly happy, thanks. And now perhaps I'd better be seeing about a wash, if you'll excuse me,' and he began to mount the stairs.

'No hurry at all. Take your own time. Tea down here in the hall when you are ready for it. We shan't be dining until eight.'

The bedroom, a vast apartment hung with faded tapestry, not only boasted a monumental four-poster bed in which (needless to say) Queen Elizabeth had slept well-nigh to the undoing of her liege subject and host, but was also furnished with more grateful modernities in the shape of lounge chairs and a settee upon which reposed the valet, a cigarette in his mouth and a drink at his elbow. 'Cheerio! I think we shall work the trick, Cyril, after all,' was his greeting. 'I don't know what it is, but there's an atmosphere about the place, which is a regular inspiration. I feel I'm going to make something of my part tonight.'

'Ssh! you can never tell who may be hanging around to overhear. If anyone so much as guessed . . .'

'It's your turn to be funky now. I don't seem to mind a bit. In fact I'm awfully bucked. Have a drink, old man, and then you'll be all right.'

'Well, pour me out just one—whew!—not too strong.' Markham spoke from the depths of a face-towel. 'Remember I've got to go and butter the old fellow.'

'You're sure little Peter's going to play up all right tonight?'

'Rather. He's frightfully pleased. Here's luck to the ghost of Cheriton Manor!'

'Here's how!' The actor raised his glass with a gesture. 'That's a damned silly thing to have gone and done—spilt your drink all over the floor. Anyhow it's not part of your valet's job to swab your wasted whiskies.'

'The glass slipped. It must have been a bit of soap stuck on my fingers. No harm done. Pour me out another whilst I mop up the mess. It won't show, it's only on the boards, not on a rug, thank goodness'

'Remember there are one or two points we have to fix.'

'Righto! I shan't forget. Here's the key of the suitcase with the initials. Your grease-paints—make-up, whatever you call the stuff—and clothes are in there. But for heaven's sake, be careful, don't leave anything about, and don't leave the case unlocked.'

'Trust me. I won't even open it until about an hour before we begin.'

'That's the best way. And now I've got to get down to the old man. Be up here at seven. I'll trot off early to dress and then we'll give it a final run over. So long.' And the door closed behind Markham.

At tea, which was taken in the hall, he found his host not only genial but expansive. It proved a simple job, simpler perhaps than he had guessed, to administer a little judicious flattery and the first morsels were so greedily swallowed that the doses became stronger and more gross. Cheriton Manor was discussed from every point of view, but chiefly they praised Mr. Fanshawe's flair in finding such a place and his shrewdness in having given so low a price for the property, although the host carefully refrained from mentioning the exact figure it had cost him.

'Really, now,' said Markham, putting down his last cup, 'you only want one thing to complete the picture—a family ghost.'

Fanshawe frowned heavily.

'I hope I haven't offended you, sir.'

'No, no,' hurriedly rejoined the older man. 'Not at all, not at all. You are a sensible fellow, and I am sure you do not believe in that kind of bunkum any more than I do. The fact is that—er—there *is* some sort of legend or other attached to Cheriton. I daresay the whole thing is pure invention from first to last. But between ourselves it is rather a sore point with me. I have always held that a man in my position, a hard-headed, sound business man, if I may say so, should be careful not to sanction—even in jest—any belief in these morbid traditions and stories of ghosts, which in their way are calculated to do very serious mischief. You may or may not be aware that to some extent I have actually come forward as an opponent of spiritualism, and indeed more than once I have expressed my views in letters to the public press and so forth. Now when I get down here and find that there is some silly gossip, especially among the older villagers, the real peasantry, I make it a point of honour not to inform myself of the details of the legend. It might conceivably interest an antiquary, but thank goodness I have always had something better to do. Curious you should have mentioned it too, because just before I left London this last time I had a few words on the subject with an old friend of mine—you wouldn't know him, Sir John Hatton, a great traveller and a very good chap, except for his—well, what I must term his extraordinary superstition. But then there's no accounting for fellows who have lived in the East, I always think. Seems to unsettle them somehow.'

'I quite see your point of view, sir,' replied Markham slowly, in the tone of a man who is obliged to accept facts rather against his will, 'the only thing which has ever given me pause, which has made me think that there may be something in it after all, is what happened once to an aunt of mine in a house in Cornwall——'

'Come, come, Markham, you'll be as bad as Hatton,' interpolated his host. 'No, never allow for a moment that the thing can be true. That's the right attitude to adopt. All the bogie stories in the world *can* be easily explained by a very few causes; ignorance, imagination, fraud, and liver, my boy, liver. Your aunt! I wouldn't accept what a woman said anyway.'

'I should have thought that it might have been interesting just to know what the story about your own place was.'

'And that's how half the harm's done. Begin by listening to these yarns—oh, many of them very clever and even plausible, I grant you—and end up by believing the whole bunch. Why, Hatton got quite warm the other day when I wouldn't stop to hear his romances. In fact, between ourselves, if I hadn't kept my temper and laughed him out of it we should have had quite a tiff. He always is a bit peppery—the East again. Here he was, ready to reel off half the history of England, and Hatton, I said, now Hatton, said I, look here, if any man shows me a ghost in Cheriton Manor I'll pay him a hundred pounds. He didn't like that. But I mean it; show me a ghost here, Markham, and I'll hand you my cheque for a hundred pounds. Ha! ha! ha!'

'A jolly sporting offer, and one I won't forget when I'm hard up.'

'Stick to your bridge, my boy, stick to your bridge' retorted the older man clapping him cheerily upon the shoulder, 'and you'll earn far more than ever you will by exhibiting ghosts I'll be bound. But now, come along, and we'll have a walk through the grounds. I like a stroll after tea, and it's quite dry under foot. We'll see the rest of the house tomorrow. Get a hat and stick.'

As they moved towards the staircase Markham paused: 'But that's a deuced fine portrait you've got there, sir. Surely a Vandyke?'

'Aha! I see you have an eye for a good painting. I took the pictures over with a good deal of the furniture when I bought the place. Of course most of the stuff was simply rubbish, but I found some first-rate bits as well. Especially the portraits. I've had a man down from town who understands these things, and he tells me that fellow over there is worth a very considerable sum; undoubtedly genuine.' And Mr. Fanshawe chuckled ruminatively as he scrutinized his bargain.

Meanwhile Black Dormer gazed down in silence with his deep blue eyes upon the purse-proud merchant whose money had bought his heritage from the last of the race. How stately and handsome he looked! One might almost have thought that a smile of infinite scorn curled those full red lips set in the pale oval face. His auburn hair, those love-locks the Puritans so detested and abhorred, fell gracefully on his shoulders, and in his ears hung two milky orient pearls. He stood, beautiful and insolent. Over his white satin doublet was negligently thrown a cloak of murrey velvet, and beneath the delicate lace ruffles an ungloved hand with tapering jewelled fingers closed upon the pummel of his sword. Through the trees, at a distance, against a stormy sky could be seen Cheriton Manor, and over it upon a scroll ran the warning *Gare à qui nous touche*.

It was the portrait that gave Peter Prothero that evening the cue for a remark which considerably ruffled their host's urbanity. It wanted about ten minutes to dinner time and the four were sipping their cocktails in the hall, the host, fussy and very much of the *cicerone*; Garraway, a moon-faced and spectacled nonentity; Peter Prothero and Markham, who in the security of the latter's bedroom had less than an hour before been settling various details of stage management and production. Fixing his monocle in his eye the little pink-and-white cherubic young man stared for a few moments at the Vandyke, and said very distinctly and slowly: 'So that's the chap who gives all the trouble, eh?'

'Chap who gives all the trouble? Really, Prothero, I don't quite follow you,' a very puzzled Mr. Fanshawe paused, his glass half-way to his mouth.

'Why yes, your family ghost. Your Cavalier johnny who walks down the staircase at midnight. That's the story isn't it?' replied Prothero with weakly smiling amiability.

'Walks down the staircase—walks down *my* staircase at midnight! Upon my word, I never heard such nonsense in all my life!'

210

'Oh, I'm sorry. Have I said anything I ought not to? But of course you know the yarn, Mr. Fanshawe, all about Black Dormer, who cut his sister's throat——'

'Black Dormer!' Mr. Fanshawe having ejaculated the two words seemed incapable of further speech.

'But of course it's all rot, and oh! I'm afraid I've put my foot in it. I say, sir, I'm most awfully sorry if I've——'

'I ought to tell you, Prothero, our host very much dislikes any discussion of these superstitions, and I am sure a ghost in his own house would quite seriously vex him,' nervously piped Garraway in a clumsy effort to turn an awkward corner.

'Thank'ee, Garraway, thank'ee,' said Fanshawe. Yes I——'

'Believe me, sir, I spoke quite inadvertently. I had no idea. Only I have heard the legend of Cheriton Manor somewhere . . .'

'Half an hour ago, my lad, upstairs; you're doing it quite well,' thought the impassive Markham watching the scene through half-closed eyes.

'And like a fool I blurted it out without thinking. I most sincerely apologize for my——'

'Not another word, Prothero, not another word' replied Fanshawe, who had quickly recovered his equanimity. 'You could not have known my feelings with regard to these matters. You never came across my letters in the public press? No?' in answer to a shake of the head from the seemingly penitent and rather crushed Prothero. 'Ah, well, then. I have no belief at all in this spookery and superstition, and when I hear of manifestations in my own house I confess I am apt to feel a trifle warm. Nay, now no more apologies, please. Let us dismiss the subject, and turn to pleasanter topics. Another cocktail, Prothero, I insist. What did you think of this morning's leader in *The Times*, Garraway, eh? Very sensibly put; now I believe . . .'

'Dinner is served, sir,' said a new voice breaking in at a most opportune moment.

During the evening the cards had gone against Markham, and several times his host and partner had not been able to control an impatient movement or a sharp tchick of exasperation. The moon-faced Garraway was a much better player too than his foolish countenance and rather cod-fish eyes would have led one to expect. Damn it all! They were down. This next hand needed close attention. Another drink? please. Don't bother, he was dummy, and he'd help himself, and make it pretty strong. Ah! that was better. He returned to his seat which directly faced the stairs. As the time drew on, he was nervous. And yet what was there to be funky about? A damned good actor, Claude, a damned good actor. Ten to twelve already. God! how his hands were shaking. He hoped nobody would notice it. He thought that chap—what was his name, Garraway—had looked at him curiously more than once. Another spot then.

Markham splashed the soda into a generous half-tumbler of spirit, and as he turned he saw the Cavalier looking down on them from the gallery. He could not repress a start. By Jove, Claude had done the thing well. The figure advancing from the deeper shadows began slowly to descend the stairs. It wore a white satin doublet, and over one shoulder was carelessly thrown a cloak of some dark velvet. The hair hung in curls upon the shoulders; there were pearl-drops in the ears. But the face! How had Claude managed it, Markham wondered. It was a miracle of make-up. It was, if anything, a bit too realistic, a bit too ghastly, the face of a corpse. The very flesh looked green and spotted with decay; the eyes sunk deep in their sockets glistened and shone with evil menace beneath the shade of the huge brimmed beaver. The lips were shrivelled like old parchment, drawn tightly back from the grinning teeth. One hand, thin, carious, almost transparent, grasped a sword red to the hilt in blood. With horrible silent steps the figure slowly descended stair after stair.

Suddenly there stole through the hall a chill blast of air, a stench foul with putrescence as the reeking breath of a charnel, and the three card-players looked up quickly from their game.

Fanshawe leaped to his feet and spun round with a hoarse animal cry of fear. When he saw the figure he staggered tugging for a moment at his collar, and crashed heavily to the floor in a fit. Garraway had collapsed face downwards over the table scattering the cards far and wide. With a still, gliding motion the Cavalier passed through the hall and seemed to melt into the shadows beyond. Gibbering and white with terror, Prothero was pointing with trembling hand at the Vandyke portrait. The figure had disappeared from the canvas, which showed a dark blank patch, and through the trees, against a stormy sky, Cheriton Manor—*Gare à qui nous touche!*

Shaking from head to foot, by a fierce effort Markham at a bound rushed up the stairs, crossed the haunted gallery and wrenched open the bedroom door. There upon the floor in the full blaze of the electric light lay the half-dressed body of Claude Heseltine. His arms were flung wide, his chin tilted up at a sharp angle, his eyes fixed and staring, and the horror upon his face was such as men thank God may rarely upon this earth be seen.

A PARTIAL LIST OF SNUGGLY BOOKS

FREDERICK ROLFE (Baron Corvo) *Amico di Sandro*
FREDERICK ROLFE (Baron Corvo)
An Ossuary of the North Lagoon and Other Stories
JASON ROLFE *An Archive of Human Nonsense*
ROBERT SCHEFFER *Prince Narcissus and Other Stories*
BRIAN STABLEFORD (editor)
Decadence and Symbolism: A Showcase Anthology
BRIAN STABLEFORD (editor) *The Snuggly Satyricon*
BRIAN STABLEFORD *The Insubstantial Pageant*
BRIAN STABLEFORD *Spirits of the Vasty Deep*
BRIAN STABLEFORD *The Truths of Darkness*
COUNT ERIC STENBOCK *Love, Sleep & Dreams*
COUNT ERIC STENBOCK *Myrtle, Rue & Cypress*
COUNT ERIC STENBOCK *The Shadow of Death*
COUNT ERIC STENBOCK *Studies of Death*
MONTAGUE SUMMERS *The Bride of Christ and Other Fictions*
GILBERT-AUGUSTIN THIERRY *Reincarnation and Redemption*
DOUGLAS THOMPSON *The Fallen West*
TOADHOUSE *Gone Fishing with Samy Rosenstock*
TOADHOUSE *Living and Dying in a Mind Field*
RUGGERO VASARI *Raun*
JANE DE LA VAUDÈRE *The Demi-Sexes and The Androgynes*
JANE DE LA VAUDÈRE *The Double Star and Other Occult Fantasies*
JANE DE LA VAUDÈRE *The Mystery of Kama and Brahma's Courtesans*
JANE DE LA VAUDÈRE *The Priestesses of Mylitta*
JANE DE LA VAUDÈRE *Syta's Harem and Pharaoh's Lover*
JANE DE LA VAUDÈRE *Three Flowers and The King of Siam's Amazon*
JANE DE LA VAUDÈRE *The Witch of Ecbatana and The Virgin of Israel*
AUGUSTE VILLIERS DE L'ISLE-ADAM *Isis*
RENÉE VIVIEN AND HÉLÈNE DE ZUYLEN DE NYEVELT
Faustina and Other Stories
RENÉE VIVIEN *Lilith's Legacy*
RENÉE VIVIEN *A Woman Appeared to Me*
KAREL VAN DE WOESTIJNE *The Dying Peasant*